"Princess Weds Killer" = Fake News

Lori Laidlaw

Published by Lynda French, 2025.

This is a work of fiction. Similarities to real people, places, or events are entirely coincidental.

"PRINCESS WEDS KILLER" = FAKE NEWS

First edition. April 18, 2025.

Copyright © 2025 Lori Laidlaw.

ISBN: 978-1998074488

Written by Lori Laidlaw.

Front Matter

"**Princess Weds Killer = Fake News**" wasn't planned. The first book, "**Lockdown + 3 Alphas = Heat**", was written as a standalone. But the main characters insist there is more to their story. For starters they got married.

Lake, aka **Tó**, is a street-savvy American Omega with a mysterious past.

Antal is a psycho criminal Hungarian Alpha. They're both wolf-shifters whose only common language is blood-lust and steamy sex.

Tó is getting Antal's beast under control but that's a work-in-progress. The two of them are *slightly* less bloodthirsty this time as they battle against shifter royalty, a renegade pack, and a false murder accusation.

Familiar faces return along with new friends, family, and foes.

HEA guaranteed.

Content Advisory: This is an 18+ adult novel involving dangerous situations. There are references from the past to off-page assault, spousal abuse, and childhood abandonment. There is violence, a killing, rough consensual sex, multiple partners, war between wolf-shifters, and dirty talk. Plus spanking and lots of sexual activity. Oh yeah, there's lots and lots of the good stuff.

Table of Contents

To the reviewer of **Lockdown + 3 Alphas = Heat** who wondered "What his older brother thought of him marrying a princess?"

Playlist:

"Bad Girlfriend" by Theory of a Deadman

"Beast of Burden" by The Rolling Stones

"Bring Me To Life" by Evanescence

"Closer" by Nine Inch Nails

"Cravin'" by Stileto, Kendyle Paige

"I Feel Like I'm Drowning" by Two Feet

"i LIKE IT ROUGH" by Lady Gaga

"In The Mood For You" by The Record Company

"Kill of the Night" by Gin Wigmore

"Little Red Riding Hood" by Sam the Sham and the Pharoahs

"Make Me Wanna Die" The Pretty Reckless

"Outta my head" by Omido, Rick Jansen, Ordell

"Piece of My Heart" Big Brother & The Holding Company, Janis Joplin

"RUNRUNRUN" by Dutch Melrose

"Sociopath" by StayLoose, Bryce Fox

"Vicious" by Halestorm

"Villain" by Bella Poarch

"Warrior" by Jaxson Gamble

"Watch Me Burn" by Michele Morrone

"Whisper" by Morphine

"Wolves" by Sam Tinnesz, Silverberg

"You're Mine" by Disturbed

Glossary

Alphabetic List of Hungarian Words Used:

alján = bottom

Államügyész – District Attorney

aludj most = sleep now

aranyos = adorable

baba = baby

baszó = fucker

bátor = brave

bocsánat = sorry

buta = foolish

cicik = tits

csinos = pretty

édes = sweet

édesem = My darling, sweetheart

én is szeretlek = I love you too

farkas = wolf

feküdj le = come to bed

feleség = wife

férj = husband

gyilkos = killer

harapás = biting

harcos – warrior

hello ki ez? – hello, who is this?

hős = hero

igen, uram = yes, sir

jó – good

kegyetlen = cruel

kis = little

köszönöm = thank you

kövér = plump

kutya = dog

lány = girl

Magyar Koztarsasag Kormanya = Government of the Republic of Hungary

mögött = behind

nagy = big

nagyúr = lord

nyuszi = bunny

olyan jóképű vagy = you are so handsome

olyan szép vagy = you are so beautiful

ördögi = vicious, devilish

ostoba = silly

piros = red

rendőrség = police

ringyo = bitch, slut, whore

róka = fox

sógor = brother-in-law

sógornő = sister-in-law

sötét = dark

szerelmem = my love

szerencsés = Lucky

szeretlek = I love you

szexi = sexy

szivem = my heart

szuka = whore

vadászgép = fighter

zacis = uncle

Kada is Killed

Beáta

If I don't control my breathing right now I'll spiral into a panic attack. My shaking body drops into a kitchen chair and I make my eyes move around the room identifying familiar objects.

Placemats, vase, microwave, air-fryer, sink. I inhale deeply and slowly through my nose then gently blow the air out past my lips. It's helping.

Professional treatment isn't an option for someone in my position so I have to rely on articles like *Quick Fix for Panic Attacks!*, the kind found in fashion magazines. Bite-sized snacks of pop psychology.

After several breaths I have to stop. The smell of blood makes my stomach flutter and the sight of it on my otherwise spotless floor makes my hands itch with the compulsion to clean. My heart-rate has slowed, and I feel much better just by breathing through my mouth.

I'm going to have to call the police, no first I need to get an ambulance. I know he's dead, but I still have to call 112 and let them sort out who needs to come here. But right now I've got to think. I've come up with a basic plan, but I have to be very exact in the words I choose, and very careful to only say what's necessary. Even though Kada is – was – leader of the Szémozsas the pack won't welcome official intrusion into our community.

Now that I feel grounded I can safely close my eyes to help open that locked box in the darkest recess of my mind. The box where I've hidden my worst memory, my recurring nightmare. I need to recall that experience vividly so I can take that emotion, the fear and pain and terror I felt back then, and use it now. I have to hurt myself to protect myself.

For years now I thought I'd buried this horrible memory for good. I had to, I was replaying it constantly day after day after day grasping for the missing bit. I can remember *before* the attack and I can remember *after*, but the *during* part is completely gone. That's probably a blessing. I hate to revisit the terrible episode now, but it's necessary. Taking a deep breath I give myself permission to remember and cast my mind back...

I step out walking fast, but still Antal crowds against me. He reaches for me, but I don't want to hold hands. I guess I gave him the wrong idea when I suggested we go for a walk by the river. He must have thought I wanted some alone time together and I do, but only to talk, not for what he wants us to do.

"Antal just stop, okay? I want to talk."

His mouth quirks in his usual tiny smile before he wraps one arm around my waist and the other across my shoulders to pull me against his chest. His lips feather light kisses down the side of my neck and I can't quiet the gasp of my indrawn breath when the sensation tingles right through me.

Angry with myself for the way I react to him I snap: "Stop trying to touch me!" and whirling around I shove him away. Of course he's way too big and strong for me to budge him, but he does step back with a confused expression on his face.

Before he can speak I continue saying: "I don't want to be with you any more. We're done, it's over, this dating thing with us is finished."

His eyes briefly widen with a hurt look before he narrows them and simply stares at me. It's really disconcerting because I expected him to question me, make demands, beg, or yell. I didn't expect this silent appraisal and I don't like it. I can tell thoughts are racing through his mind, but he doesn't say what they are. With his dark, broody looks, handsome as ever, this stillness is intimidating.

Suddenly I'm short of breath and talking too fast in choppy sentences, rushing to get the words out: "Look, I had fun, we both did, but I'm ready to move on. I mean what we had wasn't serious or anything, it was just friends hanging out and–"

"We made love, Beáta. That was more than just friends," he replies, sounding so grown up and serious.

"Well yeah, but it was just sex. I mean we're healthy and young, you look hot and I'm beautiful, so it's just chemistry, a natural reaction. Nothing more than that–"

He interrupts again repeating my words: "No? Nothing more? I asked you to marry me and you said yes. Remember?"

I lift my chin and meet his eyes with a steady gaze. "That was just a heat-of-the moment thing, nothing more. I've moved on."

As soon as I say those words I realize I've made a terrible mistake. It's as if he grows bigger right before my eyes, looming over me in a threatening manner, but in a calm, cold voice he asks: "Who? Who have you moved on to?"

Stepping further away from him I struggle to hang on to my defiance, letting my anger fuel my speech. "Well since you insist on knowing it's your brother Kada. He wants to marry me, and my parents think he's a much better match being the heir and all."

Other than his lips thinning into a taut, straight line Antal gives no sign of emotion. I feel the weight of his dark eyes drilling into me before he swiftly turns and strides away without another word. My shoulders slump in relief although my heart twinges at losing him. Did I honestly think I could keep him dangling with promises?

Blowing out a deep exhale I count myself lucky things went so smoothly. I'm still worked up though, anxious and edgy, so I decide to take that river walk and try to empty my mind. I wasn't paying attention to how far I'd walked, I later found out it wasn't far at all, before I heard a whoosh of air just as a body slammed into me knocking me to the ground.

The next thing I remember is lying face down right by the river's edge, hurting and crying and shaking from cold and fear and pain. I try to scream, but can't manage more than a low moan that luckily is enough to alert a couple of cyclists who stop and search in the tall grass until they discover my battered, bleeding, and broken body.

What happened between the first impact that knocked me senseless until I came to and was found is simply a blank. The doctors were able to piece together a supposition based on my injuries and the results of their tests. Tests like the rape kit.

My mother always told me my memory loss was a blessing. If it was so traumatic my mind refused to remember then yes... I think she was right.

I didn't need to recall the details of my beating, not when I was suffering through the agony of broken bones and having tubes in every orifice. My body was too damaged to perform any of its natural functions from feeding to evacuating.

The lacerations on my skin came from claws... and fangs.

I was brutally raped by a man, but also savaged by a wolf. At least that's what the doctors and police surmise, and I'm forced to accept what they say as the truth.

My hospital stay was a painful and lengthy ordeal complicated by a gamut of uncomfortable emotions. In addition to embarrassment and fear I couldn't stop worrying at my brain, nagging myself, striving to remember.

The memory loss left me feeling particularly vulnerable and scared. *Who hurt me? Will they try again? Who can I trust?* I didn't like being around any men, not even the doctors, so my visitors were restricted to family. My parents urged me to stop trying to remember because it was better to forget and move on. I'm pretty sure they were ashamed of what happened to me... and ashamed of me.

It was my sister, Katalin, who passed on the news and gossip making the rounds. Especially about the Szémozsa brothers. Antal had disappeared and everyone was saying he *fled the scene which proves he did it.*

Kada wanted to see me and my parents wavered before saying *not yet* so he sent flowers. He also persuaded his father, the pack leader, to banish Antal. Deco is old and easily influenced. Some same he's not just physically sick but also heartsick over what Antal did.

Kada is expected to soon step up to take his place as the Szémozsa Alpha. Their mother passed away when Antal was very young. Many people said that's why the boys were so bad, so wild. *Too much aggressive competition between siblings all vying for their father's attention. The boys were constantly fighting everyone... Had to be home-schooled... The jealousy and resentment they felt for each other made their teenage years a nightmare... Once they matured almost no female was safe.*

I lay in that hospital bed overwhelmed by the belief that what happened was my fault, that I brought this on myself. Obviously my rejection of Antal incited him into a murderous rage and this is how he retaliated.

He punished me and my fiancé by defiling my body and yet... I found it almost impossible to believe of him. As a human I don't have the shifters' sense of smell, but I'm certain I would still recognize Antal's scent – and I didn't. Unless his rage tainted his sweat with a sour odor? I can't remember so I just don't know.

Sighing deeply over the horrifying truth I eventually came to learn I'm forced to put that knowledge aside. I shudder and remind myself I can't show any doubt. It was Antal then, and it's Antal now. This is how it has to be.

Summoning the weak helplessness I felt as a teenager my tears come easily and I'm ready to call the emergency services.

"It's Kada, my husband. I-I think h-he's dead... Kada is dead! All this blood... he must be. It's... omigod I think he's killed him! Come quickly, come now!"

While I wait to hear sirens my mind returns to the soiree at the Koczinyi's earlier this evening. Word had gotten around our community that Antal was back for a visit and he'd brought an American woman with him. There'd been some trouble, I don't know what exactly because I stay out of Kada's criminal business, but the men had all been summoned to the Castle. Kada came home angry and refusing to answer when I asked about Antal.

We weren't meant to see them tonight, it was a fluke. Kada and I planned on having dinner out with friends who detoured us to the Koczinyi Castle *to put in an appearance* at a farewell party. They didn't know about the history or the circumstances surrounding Antal and us. We didn't speak to him though, because as soon as Kada saw his brother he turned on his heel to leave and dragged me out with him.

Replaying that scene can occupy me until the ambulance and police arrive. It all happened only a few hours ago. I consider my reaction and the thoughts that went through my mind.

Antal was a good-looking youth, not as handsome as Stefan but then no one was, or still is... but Antal has grown into a gorgeous man.

He literally takes my breath away. I'm still a beautiful woman, I know I am, but I also know that unlike him aging has made me I'm less than I was. I've lost the freshness that makes young girls so appealing. This Tó of his has it.

First we'd seen Csilla who was standing with Tó. I had no idea who the young woman was, we weren't close enough to be introduced yet, but the look on Csilla's face told me this girl was somebody. Her poise and sophistication coupled with that platinum hair and those aquamarine eyes, well... as a human I don't put much credence in any of these shifter claims to royalty, but this Tó certainly radiated a presence.

My friend whispers to me *this is the American girl Antal has brought for a visit*. Naturally I'm curious to learn more about Tó, but Csilla gently directs her away before we can engage in conversation.

Watching her from behind me Kada comments in awe *what a beauty!* and I sneer dismissively saying: "She's skinny."

"She's slender," he replies and I retort: "Scrawny, undernourished, and anaemic."

I don't know where this bitter jealousy came from but Kada laughs at me saying: "Sylphlike, willowy, ethereal..." words I didn't even know he knew.

"There's a rumor going around that she's a Jagiellon princess–" he begins, but I scoff at the idea saying *she's an American*.

My husband stares at the girl moving away from us. His eyes are dark with anger when he snaps: "My fucking brother better not have snagged himself a princess." I shudder at the vitriolic hatred in Kada's voice.

That's when I turned away and saw Antal. Many years have passed but... oh my heart. He is shockingly handsome, manly, and stylish. I wasn't exaggerating, I truly forgot to breath until I heard Kada huff in anger. He is determined to keep me away from his youngest brother.

Grabbing my upper arm, too rough as usual, Kada pulls me from the room. He doesn't care who witnesses him manhandling his wife in public. Dragging me down the walkway to the area where our chauffeurs wait beside the town cars and limousines he hollers for our driver.

Immediately an engine starts up and a sleek black car draws in front of us, the man leaping out to open our door. Kada shoves me inside and I half-fall on the seat with my dress riding high and showing a lot of splayed leg. My husband looks at me with a scowl before barking out an order to *cover up, szuka [whore]*. Pushing my feet off the seat he drops down heavily beside me.

He looks totally unapproachable with his arms folded tightly across his chest and his eyes staring straight forward. I can hear him snorting air through his nose like an enraged bull, and I can feel his big body vibrating in anger beside me. I can't help asking questions even though keeping silent would possibly ease the severity of his punishment. But I ask anyhow knowing I'm in for a beating no matter what I do.

"What's happening? What did I do wrong? What's the matter with you? Why did you haul me out of there without a word? We've left our friends behind, and without a ride, God knows what they're thinking... what they're saying—"

"Shut. Up." He bites off each word without even turning his head. Some men *go mental* or *see red* in their fury, but Kada goes icy cold. I recall that Antal did as well so I guess it's a Szémozsa trait.

Kada has a reputation for using his fists on his women. He's a lavish spender, but even so the current mistress only puts up with the beatings for so long before leaving him. Then he starts over again with another.

I get the dreaded, hateful strap. It's as long as a belt, but much wider. He'll either swing it like a whip or fold it in two for close-up smacking. The very first time it happened he explained that a female's punishment, as set out by pack rules, can only be administered by hand or belt to her bottom. That means from my backside to halfway down my thighs I'll be marked with welts, bruises, and abrasions.

It's always a brutal punishment because I can never meekly accept it and I fight him. That only makes it worse. As a human I'm not Kada's *fated mate*. I'm not sure I even believe in that concept, we don't have them, so a whipping doesn't arouse me the way other wives claim it does with them, the she-wolves.

This lack of arousal won't stop Kada from raping me afterwards, ignoring my pain. He considers it his right. My flesh will be battered and sore on the outside while dry and tight with tension on the inside. Both the belting and the sex are purely punishment, and very painful punishments. I believe my husband truly hates me... and I *know* that I hate him.

At approximately the same time that Beáta and Kada will have their confrontation Antal is busy disciplining Tő. He's making her crawl naked except for stockings, high-heels, and his tie round her neck like a leash to abase and belittle her.

Tő was philosophical when she told Csilla: "We both know Antal is a little bit insane, but rest assured that those same nasty body parts of his can work magic so his need to abase me is simply part of the price I pay for my pleasure."

However she doesn't share her wondering thought of: "How crazy am I that the humiliation will really turn me on?" Antal loves commanding his obedient girl, and Tó is turned on by his fiery lustful stare so their encounter is pleasurable for them both. She will also feel the pain of leather lashing her ass, thighs, and pussy, but she'll embrace the sting and her cunt will ooze wetly in anticipation of her mate's hard cock.

Tó will orgasm at last three times in the ecstasy of their coupling. Beáta won't orgasm at all.

Throughout our marriage Kada has been violently abusive in private and publicly unfaithful. In addition to flaunting his whores he belittles me for being unable to conceive. For years I accepted the failure of our marriage as my fault because I couldn't give him a child, an heir. Now I'm glad about it. He would have made a terrible father. None of his women ever gave birth so the fault probably lay with him anyhow.

Tonight jealousy broke something inside of me when I saw what a happy and beautiful couple Antal and Tó make. As soon as the car pulled into our driveway Kada lost control of his temper and started berating me before we'd even walked through the door. Our servants quickly disappeared. I wouldn't expect any help from them anyhow, they're only loyal to Kada and that's only because he's pack leader. They have no love for him or me.

He starts ranting about me *drooling over Antal* and I respond *what about you and those whores you take out instead of your wife?* He lunges forward to grab hold of me again and I jerk my body hard, stepping out of reach, but unbalancing. I stagger and fall to my knees.

I'm too vulnerable in this position. As I scramble to rise he fists a handful of my hair and begins dragging me like he's a caveman or something. I slide along the tile of the floor and as we leave the kitchen I'm able to snatch at the iron door-stopper. I only meant to hang on to it, to use it as an anchor but instead I find myself rising and swinging upwards with all my might.

The rage that's grown inside me throughout all the years of our lives together suddenly explodes. The painful episodes in our marriage bed, his cruel disdain in our daily interactions, the violence that's always simmering, and the dreaded punishments. The fear I've lived with for years gives strength to my arm's movement.

The momentum lifts me and I connect with his ear, hopeful that I've broken his head. I later learn that he suffered a *temporal bone fracture* which deafened and dizzied him before he collapsed in a coma. I don't know how long it took him to die.

I definitely lost myself into some sort of fugue state which I exaggerated for the benefit of the police. When they asked why it took me so long to call 112 I claimed to have no idea what they meant. I couldn't very well say I needed to be sure he was dead first...

"In your emergency call you said *he's* killed him, but who is *he?*" asks a very earnest-looking policewoman. I study her for a long moment and she probably thinks I'm dazed or in shock, but the truth is I'm thinking she could be quite pretty if she'd wear some makeup and style her hair.

Slowly, as if reluctant to say the words, I answer: "My brother-in-law Antal, Antal Szémozsa."

Tó and Antal Marry

Tó

I sign the register carefully since writing is something I rarely do. This is the first time I'm using Szémozsa, my married name. My signature looks childish beneath Antal's confident scrawl, but good penmanship has never been a priority.

Anyhow, it's done. We are man and wife, mated wolves, fated mates. For the rest of my life 11/22, November 22nd, will be celebrated. This is everything!

It's not so long ago that I was a desperate waif struggling for daily survival. I'd never in a million years envision this kind of Cinderella ending for me... more like Jezebel's, you know, being thrown to the dogs.

I was suffering the lust-filled haze of a heat when I first met the big handsome Alpha-hole Antal. He frightened me, yet despite that fear he drew me in, compelling me to submit and obey. A typical reaction of an Omega to an Alpha.

Then the heat ended. The terror remained, but he treated me decently so I weighed the consequences of living with or without him and the scale came down heavily in his favor. For all the times he needs to hurt my body there are just as many when he cradles me in his arms, covering me in his soothing, protective Alpha wave.

I'm a broken Omega who cannot love, I was never shown how, but as twisted as my feelings are they all belong to him. Love? maybe. Fear? definitely. Adoration? with every drop of my blood. I'm his and I want nothing more than to be his in our own lopsided bubble. And now we're husband and wife.

Last night when he knotted me was the most incredible time of my life. I recall with perfect clarity – and believe I always will – *the languid feeling that time has suspended,* from his *deep, breathe-the-air-from-my-lungs kisses* to the wonder in his dark gaze.

The piercing pain was incredibly sharp and stabbing but it soon morphed into *the most extraordinary sensation of ecstasy.* I'll never forget *the breathtaking experience* we shared as we consummated our vows. It really, truly brought *heavenly, excruciating joy.* Everything I thought, felt, and said then is just as true right now. I hug the memory close.

I wasn't really surprised when Antal told me he was knotting for the first time. Sharing the knot is a strongly emotional aspect of our mating and he's such a cold, cruel man that I can easily believe he's never felt that kind of connection before. But the experience was... truly incredible, for both of us.

He looks at me differently now. His gaze lingers over his mark at the base of my throat and I will make sure to keep my hair laying over the opposite shoulder. I want everyone to know that he's claimed me and I'm his.

Today we completed the state's legal formalities with Grigor and Maritsza as witnesses to our union. They're joining us for celebratory drinks and a meal and, hopefully! an orgy.

Devilishly I consider how we can combine it all at the same time. So long as everyone is naked any food can be used in sex play, not just whipped cream. I can be creative.

I'm just about to whisper my plan into Antal's ear so the other couple don't hear when I decide that no, it will be way more fun to just spring it on everyone spontaneously. And that's exactly what I do.

Entering our home we head straight for the dining room where a sumptuous buffet has been arranged for us.

"Oh this looks wonderful!" exclaims Maritsza. "It's the best we've ever had from our caterers."

Cook grumbled at us for hiring out but I wanted Maritsza to be part of our special day, not working in the kitchen. And we did allow cook to make our wedding cake. It's showcased on a small table all by itself and is a creamy, frothy concoction with the enticing almondy smell of marzipan. The icing wreathes round the layers in artful swirls almost too pretty to slice into. I have plans for that cake.

As we fill our plates from a tasty selection of meats, fruits and vegetables, bread and savory snacks, I casually start discarding clothing, beginning with my shoes. I unpin my hair from the fancy updo and shake out my tresses which have grown long now that I'm in good health. Reaching up to run my fingers through it I remove the clunky gold earrings and matching necklace. I love the bling but it will get in the way.

Antal pauses his meal to study me with narrowed eyes. We commune silently and that delectable half-smile lifts a corner of his mouth. Turning my back to him I gesture at the zipper of my dress and he oh-so-slowly pulls it down.

In honor of the seriousness of today's occasion I put on a strapless bra with matching panties cut high in the thigh and reaching to my waist. Antal usually doesn't let me wear anything under my clothes but he does love this style of lingerie – way more than a thong or even regular panties. It makes me feel like one of those Pin-Up Girls from old posters. This set is trimmed with a satin ribbon to meet the *something blue* wedding superstition.

I give my brand-new husband a pout with a coy over-the-shoulder look and he responds with a growl from deep in throat. Full of dark and delicious threat and promise. He turns me around so he can gloat over his possession.

His voice full of satisfied appreciation he says: "You are everything I want now, Tó, and all I want forever, *feleség [wife]*."

Lifting one of the bottles of champagne I pour it from as high as my arm can reach to splash across my chest, soaking the flimsy fabric of my bra and bringing my nipples to everyone's attention. Turning my head to Maritsza I urge her to *Hurry up, girl. It's time to play*. When she doesn't immediately react I reach over and scoop up some caviar – ugh! nasty stuff – in my fingers and fling it right onto her cleavage. She squeals *Tó!*

After a quick glance at his boss to make sure he's on board with this Grigor grabs hold of those big breasts and dives right in to feast. His girlfriend quickly strips out of her party dress and is tugging on Grigor's shirt.

Antal pulls me close enough to suck the wine from my breasts through the sodden cloth. Being Antal he only concentrates on one nipple until I'm whining at him to suckle the other one too.

Pulling back he gestures for me to remove my bra and I do so but he stops my hand when I reach for my panties. He runs his hands over the smooth satin covering my cheeks before slipping one hand around to cup my pussy. I know the material is already damp. Oh hell, I know it's already soaked and I can't blame a single drop of wetness on the champagne.

I love the wanton, decadent feeling at being naked, or almost so, while he's still fully dressed. I rub my dripping body over his expensive suit like I'm a kitten in heat. A playful wolfling who will nip and bite and

15

scratch. I'm not in heat but I am maddened by lust for my husband, mindlessly driven to be devoured by my man.

I think I moan - I know I want to - and then he flips me onto the couch, pulling me into a kneeling position. Ripping off my pretty undies he spreads my cheeks and plunges deep into my hungry pussy. I cry out *Antaaaal* as he roughly thrusts in and out, reaching deeply inside me and responding *Wife!*

"Yes, yes I'm your *feleség [wife], szerelmem [my love]*. Now fuck me like a *jó férj [good husband]* should."

In the background I can hear the encouraging voices of Grigor and Maritsza but their actual words don't reach me. I'm too far gone in the bliss of Antal's cock making me whole. I cum again and again before he even strips out of his clothes.

I love the freedom of losing control in the questionable safety of my Alpha's arms. As a vulnerable unclaimed Omega I always kept myself as silent as possible. *Don't attract attention* was my mantra meaning no moaning, shouting or screaming, and never any words uttered out loud.

From the beginning Antal coached me, using his own brand of pleasurable torments, to vocalize. Trapping me in his protective presence he edged me until I learned to release my voice. Starting with whimpers and moving up to howls until finally, the best: calling out his name, and the worst: screaming for him to *Stop!* He loves and encourages all the sounds of pleasure and pain that I make.

Antal

Never in my life did I imagine I'd become a married man. Somebody's husband. Bound together in the eyes of God and the Law. Hmmph...

Tó has turned everything in my life upside down. The sex is phenomenal, though.

We've just fucked our brains out to celebrate our ceremony at the Registry Office. Grigor and Maritsza joined us for the wedding and again for the consummation. She's a fat little girl who is full of joy and watching Grigor enjoy himself is always fun. He's always so intense. The two of them are really into each other, and I think my Beta might finally decide to settle down.

Tó likes watching, too. Grigor and I are built pretty much the same but Tó and Maritsza are opposites. When I see Grigor squeezing handfuls of all that pink flesh as his girl writhes beneath him I wonder at the contrast between Tó's sleek, slender shape and my big frame. I'd like to see how we look... later on I'll ask him to use my phone to take a video of us.

Every time with Tó is exciting but today was especially good. Maybe we'll re-enact it for the camera. She started things off by drenching her tits in champagne and I couldn't resist tasting those wine-soaked nipples. I got a little rough stripping her out of her sexy wedding lingerie but it was wet and hard to remove without ripping it. I stayed dressed except for freeing my cock to take her from behind.

There's no reason for me not be naked too, after all I have a great body that I work to maintain. There's just something extra stimulating about always keeping Tó nearly naked and ready for me at any time. And I know she likes the feeling of my clothes rubbing against her bare skin.

After fucking her kneeling on the couch I fell back and pulled her on top letting her unbutton my shirt and push it back over my shoulders. Then she grabbed hold of my unzipped pants and pulled them down my thighs. Tó's skin is cold and damp from her impromptu bath of bubbly and she presses against the flesh of my torso to warm herself.

Looking down I see her fair hair and pale skin wrapped against my darker coloring. Then she tilts her head and the lustful look in those gorgeous aquamarine eyes makes me growl with the need to possess her all over again.

Flipping us over I push my way inside her pretty pussy, wet and welcoming as always, and thrust with long measured strokes. Since I just came in her a few minutes ago I can draw things out this time. I'm raised up looking down, holding my weight off her with my hands planted by her shoulders. I like seeing her sweet tits shake each time I drive in deep and I tell her to play with her nipples. She obeys with enthusiasm, caressing and pinching.

"Use one of your hands to play with your clit," I instruct and watch as her fingers move quickly to rhythmically circle the rosy bud.

Shifting my weight to one hand I slide the other under her cute ass and lift to tilt her hips just so. I announce *there it is! when* I hit her g-spot and she goes spiraling into ecstasy. When her fingers fall away I demand she rub out another orgasm. She moves slower this time but I keep up my steady strokes and watch as her passion inevitably builds. When she bites her bottom lip to muffle her cry I give her a minute of rapid pounding forcing her to scream her release.

I'm using all my self-control to keep my own orgasm in check. Looking down at Tó's face flushed with satisfaction I order *again!* and when she whimpers that she can't I call Grigor to help while I pin Tó's wrists down.

Both my Beta and his girl hurry to join in. Still steadily stroking I watch while Grigor lazily flicks To's swollen clit back and forth and Maritsza's fingers gently tickle all over my wife's delicate skin. Tó is squirming and fighting against my hold and crying *it's too much!* but I growl at her to *take whatever your husband demands.* Her final orgasm is so powerful she brings me along for the ride and it's glorious. The four of us collapse in satiated bliss.

When Tó and I finally end up in bed tonight I'll mark her with more bites before our knotting and we'll both experience fleeting pain and exquisite pleasure as man and wife. At the ceremony the officiant pronounced us *husband and wife* and I'm pretty sure I snorted a *yeah, no.*

I will always be Tó's man, her Alpha.

Tó

I drift off for awhile, merely a moment? or minutes? and come to in a pleasant haze. My body aches, my flesh is swollen and bruised, and I'm lying in a tangle of naked bodies. My head is pillowed on Maritsza's soft tits and my cheek is sticky from the icing Antal and Grigor smeared all over her boobs. Antal shoved a fistful of wedding cake in my pussy and then licked out every crumb. I returned the favor, washing his cock in cake and swallowing it whole.

I wrap my arms around Antal's neck and he looks at me with a light in his eyes. I can actually feel the beating of my heart. I lean in for a kiss which he doesn't return but I feel his closed lips curving into a smile.

From somewhere behind me I hear Grigor get up to answer the insistent buzzing of a cellphone. That must have been what woke me. After listening to the caller he swears a bit before replying in Hungarian that Antal will phone right back.

"Grigor, what? Who was that?" grumbles Antal as his Beta drops down on his knees to look his Alpha in the eye before explaining.

I don't understand all the words but the seriousness of his tone makes me sit up. What he's saying finally penetrates.

"Alpha, your older brother Kada is dead. Gyuri says *it's urgent that he speaks to you.* You must call him right away, he is pack leader now so you must do what he says."

Antal's face is wiped blank of any expression but his eyes take on a faraway look and I think he's reaching into the memories of his past. His mind is no longer here in this room with us... with me. There's no way I can tell what thoughts are going through his mind. He's completely emotionless.

Since we just got back from a long trip we decided against taking a honeymoon. I had at least hoped for more of a wedding night celebration but hey, I've very recently learned that brothers mess with your plans and fuck up your life.

Antal stands up and I sigh with regret at losing the pretty sight of my husband's muscular body as he pulls up his pants over his deliciously firm ass, and walks away.

He calls the number back and puts his phone on speaker so we can all hear Gyuri say: "Kada is dead. He's been murdered, and Beáta is accusing you. You've got to get away, Antal. Hungary has an extradition treaty with America. The police will be coming for you."

Video Conference Call

Tó

"Antal, Réka's just come in and she's got news. Let me grab my iPad and we'll all chat on Facetime." Gyuri disconnects and Antal motions to me to get dressed while he slips his shirt back on. Maritsza has disappeared and Grigor is just buttoning up his own clothes when Gyuri's call comes in.

I only met Réka, Gyuri's wife, briefly during our visit. They have several small children and she's visibly pregnant again. It's Grigor who comments that maybe this discussion might be too upsetting in her condition and she gives a very unladylike snort in disagreement. I like her already.

"I'm the one with a connection in the police department so I'm already involved. Now Antal, hello and congratulations, maybe? I heard you and Tó are getting married?"

"*Köszönöm [thank you]*, Réka, and yes! we got married this morning," I pop my head into view on the screen. Both she and Gyuri begin talking at once but Antal cuts through all the happy chatter to ask *what the fuck is going on with Kada?* Feeling guilty at having momentarily forgotten the reason behind our call I retreat to stand behind my husband who is hunched over the table and gripping the tablet tightly.

"Okay well the police showed up at my door very early this morning to tell me Kada was dead—" Gyuri begins before his wife interrupts him.

"Actually I'm the one who answered because I was already in the kitchen having a cup of tea. This one is impatient to be born and gets very active at night so I can't really sleep, I just doze and nap."

I grip Antal's shoulders to stop him from whatever rude thing it is that I know he's itching to say. His muscles tense then ease under my massaging fingers while Réka indignantly relates how the police won't tell her anything without her husband present.

"I don't know if they were concerned about the baby or if they're just misogynistic. I think the latter from what my sister tells me. She works at the police station."

"I could hear voices and came downstairs just as Réka is ready to slam the door in the officers' faces." Turning around he speaks directly to her saying: "It wasn't a reflection on you, but I'm the next-of-kin so they had to tell me first." She again replies with that delightful snort, but allows Gyuri to draw her to his side, his arm slung about her.

"I invited the men in and they explained as much as they could. They said Beáta accused you, Antal, of fighting with Kada and killing him. You're their only suspect. But they didn't know you'd already returned to America so now that's got them thinking.

Especially since there's some discrepancy about time of death because the widow delayed reporting it. Her face is badly bruised which corroborates her claim that she was knocked unconscious. But she's claiming you're the one who hit her before fleeing. She doesn't know how long it took before she recovered enough to call for help."

"Antal I was just talking to my sister who said the timeline shows it's *possible* for you to have killed Kada before heading to the airfield. Their records show the exact time of take-off, but she said the officers think it's a stretch."

"But that would implicate Sándor and Csilla because they drove us straight from their castle to the plane. Do the police think I asked them to detour and wait in the car while I killed my brother?" he expostulates.

Réka leans in closer, lowering her voice as if confiding a secret, and says: "The trouble is László Garai is still there. He's a senior officer now and he never got over you *getting away with the assault on Beáta Majoros all those years ago*, that's what he said. Marta says he's strutting around smacking his fist into his palm and declaring he's *finally got you*."

"Antal, you weren't here but honestly the man haunted our home, had police following us everywhere, and kept raiding the compound. Officer Garai was relentless and furious at all of us for hiding you."

"You didn't hide me—"

"I know! but he was certain we did. He didn't believe we truly had no idea where you went. He subsequently learned you'd made your way to America but by then Beáta and Kada were married and she insisted the case be dropped. Dad was... well, by then he'd pretty much given up on living."

Antal speaks in a gruff tone of voice I've never heard before. "I hate that he died believing I'd—"

Gyuri interrupts: "Oh he knew you weren't guilty, Antal," just as Réka says: "We all knew it was Kada who attacked Beáta."

The news is so surprising I can't help but exclaim *what!?* And the way Antal flops back in his chair tells me he's just as shocked. "But she married him!"

"Yeah well, her family was ambitious and he was pack leader. I don't know if anyone outside of our family ever knew the truth. He couldn't hide it from us when he came home all scratched up and muddy with his clothes torn and in one of his manic moods. You remember those, right? and how we would lock him up in his bedroom until he calmed down?"

23

"I don't understand, though. I mean, you told me yourself that Beáta was in hospital for a long time and then had a lengthy convalescence at home so she must have been severely hurt... how could she have married him after that?"

"I don't believe she knew that it was him," declares Réka. "We all heard that she had no memory of the actual assault and so far as anybody knows she never did regain those missing minutes from her life. I'm sure she did remember eventually, there's no way he could have hidden his taste for violence and kept it under control, but by then they were married."

I'm a big fan of self-preservation having made numerous concessions for my own well-being in the past and even with Antal, but I couldn't understand this situation. "But Beáta is human and her family is fairly well-to-do, at least that's what Csilla said. I mean, she wasn't trapped in the marriage. Once she remembered and realized he was her attacker why wouldn't she have divorced him?"

"Because she's a shallow woman with a firm belief in the value of her own dignity, Tó. As Kada's wife she held a prestigious position, had plenty of money, servants, and a beautiful home. She'd have seen herself as *damaged goods* if she became a divorcee who'd suffered a brutal assault in her past."

"Well that's just fucking sad and I don't mean boo-hoo sad, I mean pathetic sad," I state.

"So what happens with me now?" asks Antal. "I have no reason to kill Kada. We barely acknowledged each other when everyone gathered at the Castle to fight the Fehers and rescue Tó. And I only saw him in passing before he left the party dragging Beáta with him. That was it, and we never talked.

We've never spoken since I left. Sure, he banished me, but I was already gone by then and besides it was years ago. I've made a good life for myself in the States."

"All of that's true but who would have a reason? There's always the Balázs pack but they would never attack Kada in his home. First it's heavily fortified and secondly it's just too domestic–"

"Domestic! that's it!" I shout. "It has to be Beáta. It's almost always the husband or the wife. They have no kids, right? So she's the only other possibility. And from what you've said she would have a reason to kill him."

Réka agrees explaining: "Yes, they hate each other, and for more reasons than the attack from years ago. But why would she do it now? why not years ago?"

"There's a reason, but it will be up to us to figure it out. If the police have already decided Antal is the culprit they won't be looking at anyone else."

"But there's your reason right there. Antal, she's using you as the perfect scapegoat to cover up her crime," I say and can hear the catch in my voice.

Decisively he states: "We should go back right away."

"I'm not sure that's wise, Antal. The police will arrest you the moment you land."

"I don't want to be extradited and arrive in handcuffs. We should sneak back into the country and work behind the scenes. Tó, call the prince. He said he's going back right away so see if we can travel with him. That way we'll get diplomatic immunity."

I make a face but before I can air my complaint Gyuri asks: "What prince?"

"Prince River is Tó's brother," Antal states matter-of-factly. His brother and sister-in-law just gape at them through the screen.

"Then it's true! That means Tó is Princess Lake and... and you're married to her!" shrieks Réka excitedly.

"Omigod seriously! let me tell you in the nicest way possible to fuck off with that princess-shit, okay? I refuse, refute, renounce it, or deny it, or whatever, I'm not a fucking princess."

"Well, not when you talk like that," replies Gyuri being stuffy but he can't maintain the pretense and he and Réka dissolve in chuckles and giggles.

Turning my scowl to Antal I explain: "I don't have River's number, why would I? I never want to see or speak to him again."

"Grigor has it, he keeps all the numbers for everyone and–"

Just then Grigor calls out to Antal that he's got another call from Hungary on the phone. While my husband instructs his Beta to get hold of Prince River after this call, I end the video chat with my in-laws promising we'll keep them updated with our plans.

"Okay good, and we'll let you know when we hear news," adds Réka.

"Hello, *ki ez [who is this]*?" I hear Antal say. He listens a moment then says "It's Sándor, he's heard about the murder and had the cops at his door first thing this morning looking for me."

Antal brings him up to speed with Gyuri's news about Beáta's claim. "We're returning to Hungary."

."If you're coming back both of you are welcome to stay here at the Castle again."

"Thanks but no, well maybe Tó. I don't want to drag you into our mess–"

"I think we already are... if nothing else we're your alibi."

"True, but I think it's best for me to lie low while I get this cleared up."

"Then stay at Kartal's village. My Beta has a comfortable home, I've seen it, and it's a really out-of-the-way place for you to safely hide. It's less than a half-hour away from here depending on how fast you drive."

"Whereabouts is it?"

"Just north of Tata. Driving on the E60 you branch off on a little-traveled road that ends in tiny hamlet. It's a self-contained, self-sufficient community."

"What's the name of it?"

"Oh it's too small for that! Even if there is an official name no one knows it, the residents simply call it *home*."

I look at my newlywed husband and enthuse: "Sounds like a perfect place for a honeymoon!"

Quick Turnaround Flight

T6

If I wasn't so pissed off at having to talk to River I'd find the sight of Grigor being all obsequent over the phone entertaining. He stammers and stutters out his request and I can hear my brother hesitate before taking my call.

He's probably afraid I've changed my mind and want to marry him after all. *As if!* I wouldn't marry him even if he wasn't my brother. The fact that he is just makes everything about him and the royal plans so much worse.

I clicked the speaker on so Antal can hear our conversation. He's unusually alert and engaged which tells me he's anxious. Well duh... an accusation of murder? on top of everything else he's got to hide from the police? I should be scared stiff about this situation but knowing Antal is innocent gives me confidence.

I can't resist the urge to tease the humorless young prince. "River I've been thinking about what you said..." I begin, letting the phrase dangle to amuse myself. I can hear my brother's breathing quicken and the thought of his agonized worry is delightful. Antal gives me a look that I ignore.

"What thing that I said?" he demands.

"About you going back to Hungary to claim Princess Breeze for your wife." I stop and listen to the silence at his end and I understand what they mean by a *strained silence* because the words are just hammering at the door. I'm ready to start giggling until Antal pinches me – hard!

"Uh, yes... and?"

"And I'm phoning to say me and Antal want to catch a ride back with you, on your plane. That's okay, right?" Reassured since I'm not requesting what he fears, he hurries to agree.

"Oh! Ah, yes, yes of course. That's fine, yes! We're leaving quite soon though. We like to fly at night and try to sleep for the whole trip."

I should probably resent how happy he is that I'm only asking for a ride on his jet. The relief in his voice borders on insulting... or would if I actually cared.

"Yeah it's a long, long flight. So we'll meet you at the hangar, which one is it? and what time do you want us there?"

He passes on the details and Antal nods that he's heard everything. Just before I hang up I remember to say: "Oh and River? tell your people we're coming, but don't give our names. They don't match what's on our passports." I hang up before he can argue.

"I am coming with you, Alpha," announces Grigor. "I was going to remain here to answer police enquiries but it's better if Maritsza does that. She can tell them she's just the maid and doesn't know anything."

Turning to Maritsza I ask: "You don't want to come with us? See your home and family? You do have family in Hungary, don't you?"

Before I even finish she's shaking her head with a forceful *no!* before fiercely declaring "I never want to go back. I never want to see any of them again."

My surprise must show on my face because Grigor succinctly explains: "They sold her. She's an indentured servant and lucky to come to our household instead of ending up in a brothel."

"I was very young and didn't have my *nagy cicik [big tits]* yet, otherwise..." she shudders thinking of the dreadful life she would have

29

had. Her words draw the eyes of both Antal and Grigor to her chest and Grigor caresses one breast fondly. He doesn't speak out loud but the gesture says *mine!*

Pushing me by my shoulders towards our bedroom to get ready Antal casually mentions that he's always liked big boobs. I droop until he adds "But I *love* my wife's tiny tender tits."

Happy over his words I exclaim: "Not exactly *tiny* anymore! You've massaged them into another whole cup size." And then I have to explain what I mean by a cup size. Once he understands he jokes that Maritsza *must be size Z*. Pretending to be angry I turn up my nose and announce *I'm going to pack.*

Getting to our room I discover I haven't finished unpacking yet. No point considering any of those clothes, everything needs to be washed. I upend the suitcase and scoop everything into the laundry hamper.

Knowing that I'll be spending some of my time at the Koczinyi's Castle where maids will handle my clothes I carefully select garments that won't cause any gossip. *I'm a married lady now,* I think blowing a raspberry, *and what I do reflects on my husband. Oh! I wonder if I'm supposed to pack for him?*

Before I can go looking for Antal to ask him Grigor hurries in and very efficiently opens and fills a case for Antal. He then looks at my effort and patting my hand informs me that he'll deal with mine as well.

He's doing such a good job there's no point arguing. When he spots me just standing there being useless Grigor says: "Go have a shower. No, bring Alpha to shower with you. Keep him calm, he's feeling anxious about what's going on back home."

I give him a nod and a half-smile wondering exactly what kind of monster an anxious Antal becomes. Heading back downstairs I straighten my spine and prepare to deal with anything.

Antal is staring off into space and seems unemotional until I see how his fingers clench and unclench repeatedly. I take hold of one hand in both of mine and massage gently. That pulls him out of his thoughts but when he looks down at me it's like he doesn't know who I am. I remain quiet until his eyes clear and he's able to focus again.

"To! Don't hang about, we need to get ready to go now," he chides me.

"Grigor is taking care of everything. We should grab a quick shower and change – these clothes are a mess."

Looking down at himself he then gives me an annoyed look and insists we hurry. Which we do, just rinsing off the champagne and food residue before dressing in the fresh clothes Grigor has laid out for us. Clothes that are comfortable to wear on a long flight.

Antal practically pushes me down the stairs in his hurry and just as I open my mouth to complain Grigor comes barreling down behind us with three suitcases and a laptop. He signals to us to head out to the car while he stays back to give Maritsza last-minute instructions and a passionate kiss. I know because I unashamedly turned around to watch.

The private airfield isn't far away so we arrive quickly.

As Grigor directs our driver to pull up close to the plane Antal comments: "Oh, he's got a Lear jet."

"I've heard of those... that's good, right?"

"Well... they stopped making them a couple of years ago so it isn't new. We have a Gulfstream."

I've only ever flown twice, same plane, to and from the U.S. to Hungary so I'm no expert. But as I lean over Antal to look out the car window I can see that our *(our!)* private jet is much nicer than Prince River's.

While ours is sleek with a fancy paint-job his looks old and plain. It reeks of the dull pomposity of the Royal Family. Seriously.

When we get inside it I discover that even the interior air smells like a library full of musty old leather. Or maybe it's that stale paper money odor. I don't realize I've wrinkled my nose until I see River's frown. He explains the jet hasn't been used in a while. I let that slide even though he must have brought the jet to the States quite recently.

I don't know why I'm bothering about his feelings but I reassure him saying *this is only my third flight* and *I don't like flying*.

"No, none of us do. Well, I mean no one in our... uh, my, um family likes flying."

He's only about an inch taller than me so I can easily look into his eyes to see he shares my discomfort at the meaning behind his words. We both turn away at the same time and busy ourselves with settling in for the long journey. Once we're all seated and buckled in the prince indicates that the staff can go ahead.

The engines must have warmed up while waiting for us because with River's nod we immediately start moving. I close my eyes and grip Antal's hand tightly.

"Why are you still scared? You've flown twice now so you know we aren't going to crash."

"I know no such thing!" I exclaim, gulping in a huge mouthful of air that immediately makes me hiccup. "And don't even whisper the word *crash!*" I hiss at him.

Antal chuckles and tossing his arm across my stiff shoulders pulls me in close. It's not until I feel the warmth of his body that I realize I'm cold. Snuggling in I deeply inhale his familiar scent and feel my tension ease. Except for the hiccuping that has him huffing in annoyance.

"I'll be okay once we're in the air," I say with as much courage as I can muster. Antal surprises me with a tender kiss on the top of my head.

Across the aisle I hear River's snort followed by Grigor's placating comment: "Well, they are newlyweds. They did the American service this morning."

Some time later I wake up to a dimly lit cabin with three sleeping men, all of them lightly snoring. Good thing they're sitting up otherwise the sound would be deafening.

I can't believe I actually drifted off on a plane! I guess this means I've overcome my belief that I need to be *concentrating with everything I've got to keep the plane airborne*. I can smile now at my panicked fear on my very first flight but the terror was real! Wolves aren't made to fly!

I was woken by my bladder and now I'm looking for the restroom. When I turn my head from the front to the back I see Antal is awake as well and his dark eyes are boring right into me. His upper lip lifts slightly giving his handsome face a hungry, feral look. He's turned on, probably by my fear of flying.

"I need to go," I say, keeping my voice low enough not to disturb the other two.

"Come on then," he replies standing up.

I think he's only moving out of the way so I can get out of my seat but he follows right behind me down the aisle. I turn my head to give him a questioning look but he hurries me forward with a push.

33

Antal opens the door to the tiny room and crowds me inside. I know better than to complain about him watching me pee so I just get on with it. I wipe myself and reach down to pull up my panties but instead I'm lifted up onto the narrow counter. He pulls one of my feet free from my underwear and that spreads me wide enough for sex.

Antal has already released his dick and now he roughly rubs it a few times up and down my slit before thrusting in.

"Oh hell, you've heard of the fucking *Mile High Club*, haven't you?" I grumble in accusation.

"No, explain!" he demands.

"No need, we're already doing it. We're fucking high up in the air in the restroom of a plane—" I have more to say but he hits my G-spot and my brain goes blank as sensation overwhelms me.

I don't care that my brother and the flight crew will know what we're doing in here. I don't care about anything except drowning in pleasure with my husband, my Alpha. My fingers are clutching his hair to pull his face close enough to kiss. He devours my mouth and begins murmuring the dirty insults that make me crazy with lust.

"Look at you, my slutty little Omega, so eager for my cock! So hungry and desperate to be rutted, hmm? You're just my bad, bad girl aren't you?"

"Yes, I mean no, no Antal! I'm your good girl. Please say it, call me your *good girl*."

"Sometimes," he says drawing the word out, "You are a *jó lány [good girl]* but other times you're naughty enough to need punishment. Those are the times you're a nasty begging whore who needs to be chastised, to be stuffed full of hard pulsing cock. My hard cock. Say it," he demands roughly. "Say it, scream it, tell me what you want."

"Yes! Yes, punish me with this monster," I gasp.

Reaching I shove his pants further down and gripping his tight butt pull him closer. I cup his balls while feeling his hot steely length slide in and out of me. While he gropes my tits with one hand he uses the other to yank me by the ankle into an impossibly high stretch. His eyes hungrily take in the sight of me spread wide and it's such a high knowing my eager pussy is slick and swollen for him.

Holding me like this lets him penetrate even further, driving so deep it feels painful but strangely also amazingly blissful. I'm squirming and swiveling like his cock's a corkscrew twisting its way inside me.

"Bad little Omega," he growls.

"No! Good Omega taken and ravished by the cruel Alpha. *The big, bad wolf!*"

His chuckle is a low rumble as he keeps pounding into me with fierce aggression. I don't even try to contain my begging cries of *Antal please! please!*

"Always begging for more."

"Yes! more punishment from your huge cock that penetrates so deep. You're ruining me for any other man."

At my words he turns feral with lust and possession hissing *only mine!* before slamming my hips down hard to smash my clit on his pelvic bone and I keen in high-pitched ecstasy. I keep cumming through his whole orgasm and when he pulls out he nudges something that makes me spasm again. Damn, he sure fucks good.

I feel completely boneless sprawled on the narrow counter-top, sated and sleepy. Antal dries first himself and then me with a soft hand-towel. Of course the Royals wouldn't have anything as practical as paper toweling. I smirk to think of Prince River coming in and having to use the same cloth.

There truly is no room to move about in this small space so Antal zips up his pants, kicks my panties into the corner, and pulling my dress down wraps my legs around his waist before backing out of the room.

He continues to carry me as we return down the aisle to our seats. Looking over his shoulder I see a stewardess hurry into the restroom and since she leaves the door open I know she's gone in to tidy up. I hope she's tactful enough to drop my panties in the wastebasket.

I land with an *oomph!* when Antal plops me down into my seat. Both Grigor and River are awake now. As each stands Grigor steps aside to let the prince take his turn in the restroom first.

As he walks past me River sneers with a disgusted look so I slowly lick my lips while wearing a lascivious grin. At least I hope that's how it looks although I'll settle for well-fucked.

My God if I'd had to marry him I've have lived a life of depressing misery. Without waiting to see his reaction I turn to the window. Since I can only see dark sky and clouds I curl into Antal's embrace and close my eyes for a post-coital nap.

Some hours later I waken to the sound of voices speaking low. Antal and River seem quite intense in their conversation. I can understand most of it. My Hungarian has gotten so much better with the online learning app Al the Security Tech installed for me. I keep my eyes closed and shamelessly eavesdrop.

"I'm going to be blunt Szémozsa, ah... brother-in-law, because I believe the situation is dire. Once your name was linked with Lake's my family investigated you so we know about the rape and assault charge that drove you out of Hungary all those years ago and also–"

"Alleged," interrupts Antal. The Prince is taken aback, probably no one except his parents has ever done that before.

"Oh, of course, alleged. Yes," he hurriedly agrees. "We know nothing was ever proven in court, the case never got to court, but with your brother also banishing you from his pack you unofficially became *persona non grata* here at home."

Antal doesn't protest his innocence or criticize his brother. He just calmly waits for mine to continue. In the silence I open my eyes, giving up any pretense of not listening in. River seems disconcerted if the little frown drawing his eyebrows together is any indication.

He begins again saying: "What makes your predicament even more difficult is a police officer by the name of–"

"Garai. László Garai. Pardon me for interrupting you again, Prince River, but that man... that man has hounded me and my family for years. He doesn't like shifters, barely tolerates our existence, but he truly hates when shifters and humans join together in marriage or even just friendship. He'd like to see clear lines drawn separating our two races.

The fact that I had been dating Beáta, and knowing that I'd been seen in her company the day of the attack, was enough to convict me in his eyes. He's never budged from his opinion.

Gyuri tells me Garai has already inserted himself and his prejudice into this new case, the murder of my brother. Unfortunately, it's well-known there's no love lost between Kada and myself."

River nods in agreement explaining: "This man Garai is a senior officer now and his word will carry weight or rather it would have done so if he hadn't made you a bit of an obsession over the years. He not only went after your family, he started a costly and non-productive manhunt that reached far and wide searching for you.

His single-minded pursuit should have ended when the Majoros family made it clear they wouldn't go to court, but he refused to let it go. The parents stopped him from speaking to their injured daughter, but he would hang about to waylay her younger sister with questions and demands. The father finally made a harassment complaint."

Antal's smile shows he's recalling a happy memory. He replies: "Beáta's sister Katalin was a feisty little thing. I'll bet she loudly defended me against Garai's accusations. She had a crush on me, according to Beáta, but Beáta was a jealous woman with an active imagination."

River doesn't even bother to disguise how utterly unimportant Katalin Majoros' existence is to him as he listens with a blank expression. I suppose that's better than a sneer... I guess he saves those for me.

"After word got around that you were living in America he pestered his department to apply for extradition. They refused, rightly so, because there wasn't sufficient evidence to lay charges *in absentia*. Unable to accept the decision of his superiors Garai became embittered and vengeful. He achieved higher rank through time served, not promotion, but because of his position he is a concern."

The four of us, for Grigor is listening as well, sit thinking over River's words. After a bit Antal breaks the silence thanking the prince for the information he's provided.

"Once I learned I was banished I didn't even try to communicate with my pack members, and I certainly wouldn't compromise Gyuri. It was about ten years later that he reached out to me and we were able to resume ties, although it was probably kept secret from Kada."

I can't keep my mouth shut a second longer asking: "So no one was ever arrested for the attack because the officer in charge didn't bother looking at any other suspects?"

Antal's casual response of *Remember Gyuri told us everyone knows it was Kada* blows me away. "Isn't that fucked up?" I exclaim and River wrinkles his nose at me. "Yeah, yeah I'm so *not* a princess, we all get it," I tell him, rolling my eyes at his stuffy attitude.

"That's correct, actually. So far as we can tell no one else was ever brought in for questioning. The only name on the list of suspects was yours," he confirms, turning his attention back to Antal.

"Well that crime is going to remain unsolved unless Beáta will tell the truth–"

"Oh she's always claimed to have no memory of the attack. Neither immediately after nor months, and finally years, later. Everyone has been told the incident was just too horrific for the innocent girl's mind to understand or accept. The official explanation is that the victim *blanked it out* using *selective amnesia* as *a permanent coping mechanism.* That ended the investigation."

This is obviously bullshit and I can't hold back saying so. We've all seen enough crime shows – even the news – to know that bodies leave evidence. "If the attack was that violent the perpetrator must have left behind blood, skin cells, teeth marks, strands of head hair, body hair, and pubic hair, plus the samples taken by the hospital of semen and saliva and–"

"And nothing. There is no viable DNA to match to any suspected assailant."

"Well that can't be, that's just crazy, it means…"

"Corruption, pay-offs, collusion, or maybe just plain old incompetence, call it what you like."

"Now I can see why that cop Garai is so frustrated."

"Actually no, wife. The lack of evidence should have pointed him towards someone with influence who is still here and able to pull strings, not a teenager who ran away."

What Antal says makes perfect sense and we all sit silently considering how easily the case was closed. "So his pursuit of you then and now is personal?" I narrow my eyes at him asking: "Why? What else did you do?"

He gives me the smug smirk of an egotist saying: "I used to date his precious only daughter but dumped her for Beáta."

Despite the possessiveness we each feel for the other there is no jealousy between Antal and I. Otherwise he could never share me in my heats and he does enjoy that very much. He's got a strong voyeuristic streak as well. Me? I don't care. I'm grateful for everything I get from him. I will never take my current life with Antal for granted. But, I am curious to speculate about a strikingly handsome youth *sowing his wild oats* as they say, or *fucking around* as I put it.

"If he's got this thing against shifters shouldn't he have been happy when you two broke up?"

"Oh I'm sure he was, but he was also torn between being happy for himself and angry that his spoilt girl was moping."

"She didn't like go anorexic or anything?"

"Christ no! It was only her pride that got hurt, and she was a pretty girl so she found someone else soon enough."

Leaning forward Grigor joins the conversation for the first time. "I remember her! Dorina Garai was really pretty, sure, but she had a shit attitude. Always thinking she was so much better than the rest of us because she had nice clothes and all the latest things."

"Yeah she was spoilt rotten that one. Very demanding. Not like my little Tó here who I've trained so well–"

I splutter, stumbling over the words in my haste to get them out. "Fu-fuck you, Antal!" A moment too late I realize I've gone too far.

The other two men have frozen, holding their breath, while Antal slowly turns his head towards me. He moves like a predator and his hooded gaze is threatening. In a silky voice he warns I'll be punished later when we're in a private place and the chill that shudders through me is partly fear, but mostly the thrill of anticipation. Good thing I'm his wife, otherwise I'd be degraded by feeling slutty. Instead, I'm aroused.

River steps in to break the uncomfortable silence. I guess these Royals learn diplomacy and tact at an early age. "So it looks like you're up against a racist policeman with a big ego and he's got a personal grudge against you. Strike three," he adds under his breath.

I bite my tongue to stop myself from pointing out how fucked Antal is. He's a mind reader. Without even looking at me he knows what I'm thinking and takes my hand in his to give it a painful squeeze. One look at my pale face with my lips thinned into a tight line will betray my pain but I'm smart enough not to react. The Prince pauses when he catches my expression but he doesn't comment.

"We've made arrangements to stay in an out-of-the-way place," Antal begins and when River asks *where?* my husband states it's better that our plans are kept secret. "We'll work more effectively if we can keep under the radar and I won't compromise you, Prince River."

River considers this and nods: "I appreciate that. You've got my phone number so please stay in touch. The family are waiting to hear the results of my trip and I suspect they'll want to meet."

"Well I don't want to meet— oh!" I stop as a thought occurs. "Yes, I do want them to arrange a meeting. I don't care if it actually takes place, but I'd like the gossip circuit to hear about it. I'd like word of our Royal connections to get back to the authorities."

"That's a great idea, Tó!" Grigor enthuses. Even better Antal releases my hand from his punishing grip. *Yay me!*

The overhead lights brighten and the steward lifts all the window shades signaling it's morning. I can smell freshly brewed coffee and sweet baked goods. The prince is served first and I'm surprised to be served second. Antal's huff of annoyance lets me know what he thinks about that! I hide my smirk but Grigor notices and winks at me mouthing *princess!* I give him the finger.

I eat a warm apple turnover and two buttery croissants washed down with a big cup of creamy coffee. I'm still licking the flaky pastry off my fingers when all the dishes are gathered and we're asked to sit upright and buckled in to land. Reaching for Antal's hand it's my turn to squeeze as the plane begins its descent.

I can't be sure... but I think the look he's giving me is a happy one. I stare back, drawn into the dark depths of his eyes, his mind, and his soul. My Alpha's gaze holds me pinned in place and I'm so absorbed I barely notice that we've touched down with barely a bump.

42

I've either gotten over my fear of flying (doubtful!), or I'm falling in love (impossible!), or I'm super-horny again (probably!).

The Widow is Interviewed

Beáta

My temper flares when the white SUV pulls into the driveway. How indiscreet! All my neighbors will recognize that it's a police car, even if didn't have *Rendőrség [Police]* written across the hood. *I'm surprised they don't have those red and blue lights flashing!* I grumble out loud to myself.

Heading to the front door I take a deep breath to calm down. An angry woman with clenched fists isn't the look I'm going for. Maybe I can channel this feeling later in our conversation when we discuss Antal Szémozsa? That way I can show the police that even his name invokes a mixture of anger and fear. Yes, that will work.

While waiting for them to approach I force my eyes wide open, careful not to blink, until I can feel tears forming. When the two officers step inside they'll be greeted by a wet-eyed woman visibly getting herself under control. My lips tremble as I take a shuddering breath and after a brief handshake to each I immediately clasp my hands tightly together again. As if I'm struggling to keep my composure.

I lead the detectives into the dining-room where I've set out a coffee pot and mugs. This room is decorated in a formal manner that lacks both warmth and welcome. Gesturing to the chairs the three of us seat ourselves, sitting stiffly upright.

The man says they're detectives from the regional unit and introduces himself as István Kovács, and his partner is Anikó Varga. Both detectives have serious demeanors but the stern-faced woman wears an added humorless expression of suspicion.

Kovács continues his prepared speech of condolences for my loss, apologies for disturbing me at this time, and assurances that the investigation is already well underway. After a brief hesitation they accept a hot drink, explaining that another officer will be arriving momentarily.

"Oh! Your superior officer is coming here?" I ask.

"A superior officer, but not ours," replies Varga dryly.

What does she mean by that? I wonder to myself.

"Someone you know, or knew years ago, Inspector Garai. Do you remember him?"

I lean back absorbing this information, my mind working quickly. I most certainly do remember the man, he was single-minded and driven, and he hated Antal. I let my scheming mind work out how László Garai can best suit my purpose.

Aloud I say: "I do remember him, he was kind, very kind at a difficult time for me."

Kovács looks surprised at my comment, but just then we hear heavy feet on the front steps and he goes to let the older man in. Varga remains in her chair, her face impassive but her eyes intently watching and weighing. When the two men enter the room she stands respectfully but Garai ignores her, coming straight to greet me.

Taking hold of my hand with both of his he exclaims: "After all these years! still a beautiful woman. You've hardly aged, Beáta Majoros– oh pardon, I mean Szémozsa."

Shaking his head he utters the usual phrases of sympathy. It's obvious he finds me attractive but his manner is strictly paternal and I remember

45

he has a daughter my exact same age. Her name is, um... Dorina! that's it. She and I were never friends.

Gratefully accepting a coffee he cradles the mug in his hands assuring me that: "Antal Szémozsa won't escape us this time!"

Varga has reseated herself and though she remains absolutely still her disapproval is evident. Kovács has no qualms in stating his opinion.

"Sir, our investigation is only in the early stages and we have much to learn before we can make any promises."

Gardai just leans back in his chair nodding his head slightly and wearing a smug smile. With his free hand he makes a sweeping gesture indicating Kovács can continue, but his smirk makes his thoughts about *their investigation* clear.

Both officers flip open notebooks. Kovács keeps his in hand to refer to while Varga lays hers on the table along with a pen and her phone.

Looking up she brusquely asks: "May we record?" and raises a quizzical eyebrow when I get flustered asking *is that necessary?*

Unsettled, I feel my eyes dart from one person to the other and after a moment of staring Varga simply says *no it isn't*, returning her phone to her pocket.

My nervousness puts the two detectives on alert but Garai is quick to dispel the tense atmosphere with meaningless words of comfort. Kovács face shows his displeasure at the interruption. Feeling Varga's gaze on him the two exchange a silent communication that tells me they've been partners for some time.

Varga begins the questioning by confirming what facts – time, place, actions – I gave the officers in the original interview. The younger woman doesn't attempt to dig any deeper and it seems both she and

Kovács are simply *dotting i's and crossing t's* before they put their notes away and stand to leave.

Garai follows suit, finishing his drink and loudly smacking his lips. He's puffed up with self-importance at having de-escalated the situation, but I'm not fooled. I know the detectives will be back without the older man running interference on my behalf.

Kovács and Varga have no intention of coming back to the Szémozsa residence. They will tell their boss what happened and ask to bring Beáta Szémozsa to the station for questioning on their turf. It's Károly Horváth they answer to, not László Garai.

Back in the car Kovács expels his frustration with a few choice swear words adding: "What a waste of time that was, Anikó."

"Actually we did learn something important, István Kovács." When he turns to her with a questioning look she explains: "The widow is very nervous about the statement she made. She's going to claim she was stressed at the time and can't be held to account for anything she said while in shock. But now, now that the danger and the initial trauma has passed, she knows her words will be examined closely. She refused to be recorded. Beáta Szémozsa does not want to be startled or angered or maneuvered into saying something she later regrets."

"Do you think she killed her husband?"

Looking back at the house where Garai is squeezing Beáta's shoulder and making a lengthy goodbye Varga replies: "I'm keeping an open mind... unlike that old fool."

I thankfully close the door on Senior Inspector Garai and his wild promises of retribution. I'm glad to have him on board, but he's such a tedious man.

Casting my mind back to the time of the assault I recall how certain I was that this veritable bloodhound would track my assailant down. Of course I never actually believed it was Antal because I knew his body quite well. And despite his reputation, and the volatile temper that caused it, I'm sure he would never have hurt me with such brutality.

With my thoughts firmly lodged in the past I drift back to the dining room and sit down. I'm thinking of the time before the attack, when Antal and I were lovers and in love. He was a notorious *bad boy* and I craved rebellion. The two of us burned up in the passion of our teenage love affair. We each felt a magnetic attraction that kept us glued together at the lips in public, and delighting in the discovery of sex in private.

My parents tolerated him, expecting our youthful fling to be short-lived, but Antal's single-minded drive and handsome good looks kept me in thrall. His father's reaction to us was lukewarm.

I later learned that he didn't see me as a Pack Leader's wife and apparently he'd chosen his third son to fill that role. The problem wasn't just because I'm human but because I wasn't Antal's fated mate. Deco knew from personal experience how fulfilling marriage to one's fated mate could be, and that's what he wanted for his boys. I never believed in that fated mate nonsense.

Having me visit their home meant I was often in close contact with Kada who exerted all of his considerable charm. I was just a young teen, an inexperienced girl easily mesmerized by my boyfriend's sophisticated older brother.

I remember an occasion when Kada absentmindedly picked up my hand making my fingers tingle with a shock like electricity. When I jerked free he was full of apology explaining *I wasn't thinking when I reached for you... it just felt so natural, so right.* I agreed until Antal roughly pulled me away. From the black look he wore he was itching to drive his first into Kada's smirking face. Instead, he settled for some cursing until I frowned at him in disgust. Kada grinned and gave his snarling brother the finger behind my back. They didn't realize I could see them in the mirror over the fireplace.

The very first time Kada appeared on my doorstep my family gave him a warm welcome. I succumbed to Kada's manipulative performance, aided by my parents approval. The Majoros had breeding but little else so the heir to a thriving pack was seen as an excellent match.

Lifting the mug to my lips I'm pulled back from my rambling thoughts by the bitter taste of cold coffee. No more daydreaming! I need to keep my wits about me, to stay alert and sharp. I won't get out of answering questions for long. Sympathy for the shocked, grief-stricken widow will fade.

I berate myself now for ever accusing Antal of killing Kada, accusing him of fratricide, but how could I have foreseen him leaving the country so quickly? If he'd flown out the next day it would have looked like he was fleeing and people would be convinced of his guilt – just like before – but now... now there's a huge discrepancy.

My word could have stood up against his, particularly if I *suddenly regain* my memory and accuse him of the near-fatal attack all those years ago. But my word against the Koczinyis? and a driver and a pilot and Antal's new girlfriend? No way.

But maybe it will be okay, I muse. With Antal safely tucked away somewhere in America there's no need for anyone to defend him because no accusation can be brought. It will be just like my assault all over again. I pulled it off then and I can damn well pull it off now. The thought comforts me.

Kartal's Village

T6

It feels good to get off the plane, to stretch our legs and breathe in fresh air. It's crisp and cool without a breeze.

The rental car Grigor arranged is waiting for us but it's not our usual type of ride. It's a small sedan and he's scowling as if it's personally offended him. I don't know what Antal says to him, I'm still learning swear words and slang, but it makes River laugh. He has a sports car waiting, an older classic model. Grigor's face brightens as he admires the vehicle.

"I like it," he says, "but I preferred the Lamborghini, Prince River."

"Yes, I enjoyed driving that Aventador but I doubt I'll be able to import one here. This old girl has been good to me for many years now. She's reliable and comfortable, but it's getting hard to find parts."

Before Grigor can launch into a story of his own Antal steps forward to shake the prince's hand with thanks for the flight. I'm not ready to be friends with my brother but I acknowledge the help he gave us with a nod. We're already driving away in our cars before the flight crew has deplaned.

Antal put me in the front so he can spread his legs across the rear seat. Here they drive on the same side of the road as back home. I never had any desire to learn how to drive because the traffic is always so busy and car ownership was never a possibility for me. But here... I think I could manage to drive on these sparsely populated roads. Roads with only two lanes instead of ten.

My mind drifts to the day and evening Antal drove us to a favorite spot from his childhood. We picnicked by the water then cuddled and drank Pálinka under the stars. He had to do all the driving which was risky since it was a tipsy ride back to the castle.

Looking out the window at the passing scenery I see the same type of view we saw before. There are few signs of habitation. After skirting around a city we continue through wide-open countryside with Grigor counting off kilometers. He has a puzzled look as he slows the car right down before turning down a stony dirt road that's really more of a lane or even a pathway. Narrow and overgrown with weeds it twists and turns, seemingly leading no where. Bushes brush the sides of the car as we bump along looking around in each direction.

I spot smoke and soon we can see a chimney in a red-roofed house. More of the whitewashed homes appear with most having the same type of roof but some are thatched roofs. It all looks very isolated, insular, and rustic.

"There aren't any cars around," exclaims Grigor.

Antal replies "No wonder they don't care about the condition of the road. I see carts and there, in that field, those are oxen."

"You mean bulls?" I ask uncertainly.

"No, oxen. They're very strong but calm creatures, easy to manage, good for pulling carts," Antal explains.

The animals lift their heads to stare at us just as all the people come stand in their doorways looking out and waving. I'm surprised at the number of inhabitants, and to see so many younger ones along with plenty of children who dart after our car.

One elderly man hustles towards us with a bowlegged gait and a cheery shout. Kartal has arrived already the old fellow, his *zacis [uncle]*, tells us. His dialect is thick and I can't decipher the words but Grigor has no trouble understanding despite Uncle missing most of his teeth. He gives directions to our temporary home which seems to be at least a mile distant.

We arrive at a much bigger home and Kartal is waiting with a big grin. I'm sure everyone in a wide vicinity can hear when a car approaches since it's so quiet and still. The only other structure I see is an ancient ruin, a castle or monastery, which the dirt road doesn't reach. We'll have plenty of privacy.

Kartal is an exuberant host, delighted to see us and giving welcoming hugs and kisses all round.

"Come in and warm up, we're having colder weather than usual this month. Meet my staff who will make your stay so comfortable."

Duna, his housekeeper, is an attractive young woman as are the two teenage maids, a pair of sisters called Kinga and Ilka. They moon over their master with dreamy eyes and I'm sure Kartal always has a bed partner and probably more than one! He's a different man in his own milieu as head of the house. Here he's confident, manly, and very much in charge.

"I'm honored to invite you three into my home and you must stay as long as you please." Turning to me he advises that Csilla will be here tomorrow morning. "She'll take you back to the Castle and she's already lined up some people to speak to as witnesses including Marta, Réka's sister."

I nod remembering that Antal's sister-in-law oh! my sister-in-law now too, has a sister working at the police station.

Kartal goes on to explain: "Antal, you'll need to stay here while the investigation goes on but be assured we'll take care of you."

I squint my eyes narrow at the pretty servants knowing Kartal's charms are nothing compared to Antal's rugged handsomeness. He rumbles at me and when I look up his expression shows amused exasperation.

In halting English that the women can't understand he states: "If you drain me dry and fuck my cock raw tonight *csinos feleség [pretty wife]* you can leave without worry or jealousy."

"Maybe I'm worried about them and all the damage you might inflict on that young flesh," I retort.

Antal gives the giggling girls a speculative look before meeting my narrowed eyes. Duna is voluptuously built but she's blonde, not his preferred type to abuse.

He smirks and explains: "Tormenting your body gives me everything I need, my mate. I will show you exactly what I mean later."

Laughing, Kartal agrees Antal can get his wish because he's made plans for us.

Of course he has...

Shifter Night Life

Antal

Tó is intuitive. I used to think her silence and distance were born of fear and to an extent that's true, but she's also highly attuned to the people around her. She probably learned that as a survival skill. Right now she's sensed that I need some time on my own with my thoughts so she's gone off to the kitchen with the young women and I can hear their quick-speaking voices and laughter as comforting background noise.

The looks Kartal has been giving me indicate he'll happily abandon the outside work he's doing if I want conversation, but he's respecting my position as an Alpha and leaving me alone.

So I'm free to untangle the conflicts I'm feeling now that I'm back in my homeland. We were just here days ago but that visit was for an urgent purpose. We needed to join the fight against our enemies the Fehers, a human gang encroaching on our territory. They began with damaging property but that soon escalated to violence.

As soon as we resolved that problem I happily headed back to the States. Things are different this time. Yes, there's still a specific purpose for the trip but the mission to clear my name has become entangled with feelings of how I identify with my birthplace.

On Prince River's jet I was struck by the sense of coming home. It felt like I'd been on a long journey, one that started when I ran away as a teenager, and am now returning.

Even though I ended up meeting with both of my brothers on the first trip it wasn't in the least bit like rejoining my family. In fact, I felt completely out of place.

This second trip, to clear my name, makes me realize that I do want to take up my place here. Probably not permanently, I've built a business and a life in America, but I know in my heart that Hungary is still home. I want to publicly acknowledge and be acknowledged as a Hungarian, and as a member of the Szémozsa pack.

Gyuri is Pack Leader and his son will eventually follow him. I have neither the inclination nor the ambition to challenge any of that, but I do long to be among my own kind. Fellowship, camaraderie, blood ties... I hear the call.

Plus, there will always be threats to the alliance and I want to be part of the solution. Just as I want to travel across the country showing Tó the beauty of Hungary, the warmth of its people, the comfort of a slower pace of life. A sky full of a billion twinkling stars.

The sun is setting so time is moving on. Kartal has glanced over at me several times and I know he has plans for us tonight. I see Tó come to the doorway but remain standing there, patiently waiting for me. Then she smiles and I feel the magnetic pull of her allure. Why do I find her so irresistible?

I think back to our first meeting when she was just a scrawny, beaten-down Omega who went into heat. We had some fantastic fucking but it wasn't until the next day when she showed so much courage despite being petrified with fear. She accepted her fate but not with morbid resignation, no, she accepted and consented to an adventure.

To this day seeing that proud, stubborn bravery when faced with my depraved needs drives me crazy with desire. I ache to break her, enslave her, ravish, and adore her.

I motion to Kartal that I'm heading in and he hurries over to walk with me.

Tó

"The villagers are thrilled to meet a princess and wanted to host a dinner but I told them that won't be possible," explains Kartal. "You've had a long day of travel *and* it's actually your wedding night. So instead, they will give you breakfast with a quick visit on your way out tomorrow morning."

"How do they know I'm a princess?" I ask Kartal. My hands are fisted on my hips to show my displeasure but he has the nerve to laugh!

"It's big news in our community and even some of the mainstream outlets have picked up the story from social media streams."

I've been receiving unwelcome publicity as the long-lost daughter of Hungary's ex-Royal Family, still honored as shifter nobility.

Looking at the three men I ask: "Who are these people? I know some of these Internet news sites aren't even Hungarian so what's it to do with them?"

Antal has to slip back into his native tongue since his language studies haven't advanced as quickly as mine. He speaks slowly so I'm able to understand. "The Internet empowers those little people who don't otherwise have a voice."

"You mean the losers living in their mother's basement–"

He interrupts exclaiming: "No! that's a generalization too many people use and I believe it's a false and foolish one. No, these people call themselves *Social Justice Warriors* and they strive to right wrongs by shining the spotlight of social media on injustices."

"But there is no injustice here–" I begin but again he cuts me off.

"Tó, of course there is. Your family abandoned you to die for no other reason than their elitist pride. And when they discovered you'd survived against all odds they came after you with murderous intent."

The trauma that was inflicted on a 14-year-old me once again invades my mind. My body trembles with the same panicked fear I felt then and I reach to grasp Antal's hand.

I'll never erase the memory of fighting for my life against a vicious, violent attack from snarling wolves, their foam-flecked muzzles spewing insults about *the runt of the litter, weak and sickly, polluting the bloodline*. Years later my twin brother the prince tried to placate me saying *it's true you were abandoned but only because they felt you wouldn't be able to produce a healthy heir*. I wanted to kill him for speaking as if that explanation was perfectly reasonable.

The anger rises within me again until Antal pulls on my hand to draw me tight to his chest, crushing me in his strong embrace until the shaking stops.

"Tó, my sweet Tó don't be upset. Not by this. Save your pain for me, you know I relish it."

I give a weak laugh at his words even though we both know he isn't joking. My husband truly is the devil in the disguise of a stunningly handsome man.

He continues saying: "You know you don't have to do or say anything, not unless you want to. If there's nothing new to the story it'll die and eventually these people will find a new cause. As for your family, well hopefully they'll drop it and go away."

"But what it they don't?"

"Then we'll find them and bite them–"

"Oh yes! We'll bite huge chunks out of them and toss the pieces in the trash. No, in the gutter. This time I'll put *them* in the gutter."

"We'll all help you to do so," confirms Kartal, his tone ending that discussion.

"Tonight we have a strong moon, not quite full but very bright, so we'll shift for a run. The girls love to be chased, well what they love is being caught! and Antal what better way to celebrate your marriage then hunting your bride in a heart-pounding race through the forest for a claiming bite?

Tó, I know you loved your one taste of primal play so I'm hoping this plan works for you?"

I'm enthusiastic for another outdoor experience, and when I see the fire in Antal's eyes I know we'll indulge in rough, passionate sex. All traces of tiredness from the journey vanish at the thought of running wild and free.

Duna leads us into a dining-room where the table is already set and laden with food. Antal insists I sit in his lap. The talk turns to teases about eating well to keep our strength up for the night's adventure! The bawdy toasts, the spicy dishes, and the strong red wine soon get us in the mood for a lust-filled romp in the woods.

Grigor responds to Duna's flirtatious winks by pulling her close for a kiss before smacking her behind. I'm reminded of how often I've seen Maritza with a red bottom after being sent to the Beta for a disciplinary spanking. Afterwards she gets the same kind of smile on her face that Duna is wearing now.

I'm sorry Maritsza isn't with us now, but I can't blame Grigor for sampling Duna's charms, he is an unmated wolf. For now, that is. Duna and Maritza share the same curvy figure of all good cooks so he definitely has a type.

Kartal suggests we leave our clothes in our rooms and shift before going out. That's a good plan. I'm just enjoying the free feeling of my wolf self when Antal's jaws catch the back of my neck and force my head down to the ground. He snuffles in my ear and sends telepathic thoughts of how he's going to savage me when I'm caught. *If I'm caught!* I send back and his answering growl sounds like a laugh before he releases me.

We try to maintain some decorum as we stalk outside finding the others ready to go. The young girls have sleek brown coats while Duna's fur is quite blonde. The coats of the male wolves are all familiar: Antal's dark gray, Grigor's distinct red, and Kartal's black. The six of us make a handsome pack.

At Antal's signal to *Run, Omega!* I go, but let the other women move ahead to lead the way. Once we're under the cover of the trees we'll shoot off in different directions to make the men work harder.

Kartal told us that on a night like tonight we'll hear other wolves out and about but our part of the forest is private. He's right about the brightness of the moon. I can clearly see the three racing in front of me before they melt into the darkness of the woods. The last I saw of the sisters they went right and I'm pretty sure Duna veered off to the left so I plow straight ahead.

I'm immediately enfolded in the warm and vibrant ambience of the forest with its peat and pine smell. The air is alive with a variety of sounds: the chirps and cooing of birds nesting for the night, rustling leaves, humming insects, and the stealthy padding of other animals' paws.

Far off in the distance I can hear a number of wolves on the run. They're howling and barking and reveling in the freedom of darkness and camaraderie. As usual when I hear the excited yips of the younger animals it reminds me of children's laughter. A warmth spreads right through me, filling me with comfort and contentment.

My senses lull me into pleasant relaxation as I run at an easy pace so it's startling when an alpha wave reaches for me. Luckily it's still faint enough that I escape being knocked to my knees, but now I'm warned that Antal has caught my scent. My wolf mind doesn't think in words, instead it reacts to sensations. It senses my Alpha's lusty aggression just as he will feel my fearful anticipation. I'm on full alert as I flee away from his powerful pull.

Darting between trunks both thick and thin, rushing through chest-high ferns and leaping over boulders I thrill at the freedom of running. The breeze I create riffles through my fur, my nerve endings awaken, and I'm driven by the hot blood pulsing through my veins. I'm exultant with the high of being a wolf as I swerve, change directions, crawl into the undergrowth, splash through a stream, and finally trot into a clearing. The grass here is soft on my pads and I pause to steady my breathing while I cock an ear to listen.

Silence.

A perfect opportunity to fall back on this verdant lawn to scratch my back then sprawl for a rest. I look up at a million billion twinkling stars and once again am reminded of our romantic night at the ruins. Stretching I luxuriate in my fully engaged senses.

Antal's stealth is a testament to his superior hunting skill when he pounces, catching me completely unawares. I twist sharply in terrified reaction and manage to slip from between his front legs. My panicked escape only lasts a moment before I'm brought down as he crashes into me with his full weight. I'm captured by a captor who is primed to rut.

I should have recognized the silence as a warning signifying that a predator lurks nearby. I still have a lot to learn as both a human female and a she-wolf.

The big gray Alpha wolf wrinkles his snout which lifts his upper lip in a fearsome display of fangs. His eyes are hooded and his growl is fierce. I've swiveled on to my back offering my throat and belly in supplication. He commands me to shift and of course I obey but I'm terrified as I lie trapped in the body of a helpless woman beneath this feral beast. Antal's eyes narrow to slits as he throws back his head and howls. His call his loud and proud.

The red wolf, Grigor, rushes into the clearing with the blonde wolf trotting close behind him. Kartal arrives shortly after with the two slim wolves playfully nipping as they leap around him. Their excitement evident in their yipping cries. They quickly circle their Alpha and I can hear their panting and feel their hot breaths but I don't dare take my eyes off Antal as I'm surrounded by this makeshift pack.

I'm bathed in the pale color of the moon that shines like a spotlight on my naked body. The barely restrained violence of the animals is as intoxicating as it is terrifying. They can scent the arousal that has me squirming and they hear the rapid beat of my heart. I'm delirious with a tsunami of powerful emotion but Antal spreads me wide with his forelegs before shifting back to claim me in human form.

The pack watches as my husband forcefully fucks me with snarls and declarations of *MINE!* He manhandles my legs, pulling them wide then folding them up against my chest so he can penetrate deeply while pinning me down. He's rearing over me and all I can reach are his hands holding my ankles. I'm incoherent as I gasp my pleasure at the waves of ecstasy rolling over me.

I'm going to feel the ache from head to toe tomorrow after this rough pounding on the ground but right now I'm determined to prove I can take it. This is my battle to win. I sense the pack's approval at the savage way their Alpha is mating his Omega and I'm damned if I won't earn their admiration too.

Antal climaxes and roars at me to shift back again. This time he remains a man holding tight to my silvery fur. I'm much stronger in this form and we wrestle competitively with rumbling barks and growls and when his cock turns to steel he turns back into his wolf. Now we can let loose our untamed, ferocious natures.

Antal mounts from behind and locks into me, making me spasm with contractions that drive him mad with rapture. There are no kisses, cuddles, or caresses in our wolf form. There's just the power of his weight over mine, the threat of his jaw holding my neck, and the strength of his alpha waves commanding my submission. I nip and he bites. I give a keening cry while he howls again and again and again.

I'm vaguely aware of the others moving away to enjoy their own mating but I couldn't say if they are now humans or still animals. The guttural groans and the *ai ai ai* cries sound the same in either form.

We shift, we shift again, we revel in the gift of our dual nature. We wolves are swift and strong with finely-tuned senses. We're hunters and predators. We mate for life but... we play games without rules.

And I am no longer prey.

Sated I push against my Alpha wolf sharing his warmth and matching the rhythm of his breathing. In this form we don't talk, we're content to watch the others indulge themselves.

Duna is an Alpha and her dominant streak shows when she shifts to escape Grigor who quickly changes back to a man. Duna straddles his big body and pressing her hands to his chest pushes him to the ground. With her feet flat on either side of him she gets the necessary leverage to push up and down on his cock. *Her legs must be super strong!* I think, seeing how they accordion.

She's a fit young woman and her large size is solid, not flabby. Grigor is giving her control, but soon enough she'll be flipped onto hands and knees while he fucks her in his preferred position.

For now he's mesmerized by Duna's big boobs swinging in his face. Lifting his upper body off the grass he shoves his head forward so he can smother his face with her pillowy tits.

A murmuring that reverberates through Antal's chest tells me he's watching intently and once again I wish I was busty. I must have sighed because my mate senses my sadness. Bending his muzzle to hold my neck he drenches me in an Alpha wave. My mind clouds as I'm enveloped in a powerful sense of his satisfaction. It strengthens me so I lick his paws in gratitude.

The slender brown wolves frolic over Kartal's wolf, rolling over and under him, darting in to nip then pulling back to tease. If he chases one the other butts him from behind and when he turns the two pounce. Their arousal is turning vicious and now the nips are accompanied by squeals of pain and drops of blood.

Before the she-wolves can hurt each other Kartal shifts and orders them to do the same. He laughs, they giggle, and the tension breaks. Kartal is a big guy and the girls swarm all over him, their lithe young bodies twisting sinuously around him. Without clothing to distinguish them the sisters are very much alike. Maybe they're twins?

I'm awed again at the recent discovery that I'm a twin. I've never felt like one. I mean, I've read about other twins who were split up at birth and yet they still knew they were a twin. Maybe that's all bullshit because it never seemed like a part of me was missing or that I was lacking something or someone in my life. River... my brother. Prince. I shake those thoughts away and concentrate on the playful antics in front of me.

The three of them are kissing, licking, and sucking to the accompaniment of begging, squealing, and gasping cries of need and pleasure. Hands are all over each other and on themselves, too: rubbing, stroking, pinching, and squeezing. One girl is holding out her tit as an offering to Kartal's lips while the other girl caresses his balls and slips a finger up his ass. He reaches down to cover each girl's pussy with his big massaging hands.

I feel Antal's teeth running across the base of my neck and I shiver with desire. We're both enjoying the sex show, both of us voyeurs at heart.

It's fun to watch them but the long day has finally caught up and I can't stop my jaw-cracking yawns. Antal nudges me upright and without a word we turn homewards. Starting with a trot we're soon loping then running as we race each other. We hear the younger ones struggle to overtake us, but they don't have the stamina and even I fall back when Antal and Grigor outpace everyone.

The males are impressive in size and speed. They run so swiftly yet so easily. I feel my mate's pleasure in the strength of his wolf body, and in the freedom of a wolf's life.

By time I reach our room I'm exhausted though exhilarated from our nighttime hunt. Antal is naked, all his tattooed muscles on display to my appreciative gaze, as he sprawls on a hand-carved wooden bedstead. I just know that the soft, puffy mattress he's sinking into is feather-down.

I feel my mouth stretch wide with a joyous grin when he seductively invites me into his arms: *"Feküdj le [come to bed]."*

And I comply saying: "*Igen, uram [yes, sir]!*"

Trial Separation

Tó

Not long after we climbed into the comfy bed a booming sound woke us and I realized it was thunder. Sheet lightning brightened the night sky followed by a heavy downpour. Lying cuddled together in our warm bed listening to the storm was the most comforting thing I have ever experienced. Such an overwhelming sense of safety and well-being.

"Some day, or night, I will take you out for a hunt in the rain. I'll chase you down and have my fun dirtying my *aranyos nyuszi [adorable bunny]* in the mud."

"I'm no bunny," I sleepily protest. "I am your *szexi ringyo–*"

"Bitch?" he asks, surprised.

"Well I meant *slut* but I can be your bitch if you like..."

"No, I like slut, I like *sexy slut*. Tó is my *szexi ringyo.*"

Antal untangled his legs from mine before bending my knee to pull me sideways onto his erection. This is my first time in this position and it's a lovely, lazy way to screw. He holds me with one hand on my tits, the other pressing my clit, and his mouth on the back of my neck while he gently pumps his hips. I really can't do anything except accept the pleasure of his touch. When he starts moving his fingers faster and his cock deeper I surrender to his ownership of my body and... and my heart. It is our wedding night, after all.

Even the crack of lightning can't mask the high-pitched yelp when I orgasm. Antal's rumbling groan makes me giggle saying: "That one was close by!"

I'm usually the first to fall asleep, often blacking out after orgasmic sex, but tonight a question pops into my mind.

"Antal, why did you move to America? Why not choose Canada? I've always heard that it's much friendlier to wolves there."

"I wanted to avoid wolf packs. Remember Kada banished me and a lone Alpha, ostracized from his community, isn't welcome anywhere."

"So you were on your own, living as a human only, for... how long?"

I feel him shrug as he answers: "Just a few years. Grigor pestered Gyuri until he revealed my whereabouts and then he made his way to be my Beta."

I hesitate, afraid it might be a too-sensitive subject, but finally I remark: "Grigor is in love with you."

"Mm-hmm, he is."

I turn in his arms to see what expression is on his face. As usual his countenance is blank. He could be a Grand Master on the poker circuit, if there is such a thing.

"I mean, he loves you as a man, not just as his Alpha or even as a brother."

"I know."

Ugh! he's so frustrating. "Well... what about it?"

"Just come out and say what you want to say, Tó. Do you want to discuss our past sexual histories? You've always avoided the topic before."

"No, I don't want to talk about me I want to talk about you. You and Grigor."

"Are you jealous of him?"

That does make me pause as I think about it. I realize that no, I'm not jealous of their relationship now so I shouldn't care about whatever it might have been. During my heats I've fucked Grigor myself so...

Antal has several handsome friends, drop-dead gorgeous actually, meaning it's likely he's been bi for some time. And that's okay. In fact... I wonder if it's usual among wolves? There's so much about my heritage that I just don't know.

Reaching down I take hold of his cock and trying to mimic his voice I declare *Mine!* Chuckling, he pushes my head down and since he just came I know I'll get to play for quite awhile. He isn't rock-hard so with a bit of work I can draw him down my throat before pulling my head all the way back along the length of him.

Antal runs his fingers through my hair and murmurs: "So long as I have you with me my world is big enough."

Antal

Csilla arrives in the morning while we're meeting the villagers. Everyone admires the big shiny car and they're suitably impressed to see a uniformed chauffeur. These simple people don't need to know that he's also Csilla's bodyguard.

"Sándor wanted to come, he's got lots to tell you Antal, but there's some trouble brewing so he has to stay at the Castle."

It's obvious Kartal wants to speak but he defers to the Alpha.

"Will he be able to talk on the phone about it?" Antal asks.

"Oh I think so, I don't believe it's confidential. Just news and rumors and possible leads. Yes, Kartal?"

"What kind of trouble? am I needed back there?"

Csilla frowns before slowly answering: "I think we'll all need to be back there to deal with it, but for now we're just waiting. So, in the meantime, we can work on disproving Beáta's false accusation."

Tó brought her suitcase along with us when we left Kartal's so she's ready to go just as soon as we finish breakfast. Every household has contributed something making this quite a feast. I love watching my wife eat. She still has a voracious appetite and the villagers are flattered, marveling at the amount of food she puts away.

The one and only time I teased her about it she snapped *try going hungry, with only filthy scraps from dumpsters to eat, and then you can judge how greedy I am with good food.*

I remember feeling ashamed of myself but I could never admit to that and instead told her to *eat my dick.* I smile now at the memory of how my little spitfire broke into a slow, sexy smirk. She won't say anything snippy to these country folk who are delighted that she's sampling everything and even having seconds.

After another hour has passed we're ready to go our separate ways. Kartal and I will go back to the house, while Grigor will accompany Tó back to the Castle with Csilla and her driver Máté.

l narrow my eyes at Tó but she knows I'm teasing when I say: "Only married one day and already living apart!"

I'm all about presenting a stoic front but not my wife. She jumps up to fling her arms around my neck and seek out my mouth for a lengthy, passionate kiss. I feel my lips quirk into a tiny smile before murmuring: "Be my *jó kislány, feleség [good girl, wife].*"

She answers quite properly, although I suspect sarcastically, "Yes my Alpha, my *férj [husband]*, my *sötét nagyúr [dark lord]*." I must be smiling because I'm rewarded with answering grin from her and a quick goodbye hug.

The other three have been patiently waiting in the car for us to finish our farewell so I apologize. Csilla says: "Oh, no need Antal. I love seeing this side of you that only Tó brings out. The drive will give us enough time for me to hear all about the wedding."

Grigor's expression is a smirk as he relives his favorite memories from the wedding but he won't be sharing those reminisces with Csilla.

A New Threat

Antal

When we return home from the village Kartal leads me to his office where he places a video call to his Alpha, Sándor. Once the connection is made he gives me his chair but stands behind to remain part of the conversation.

"Antal! I'm glad you've arrived back safely but sorry to add to your worries. Those bastard sons-of-whores in the Balázs pack are using the distraction of your situation as an excuse to attack our business."

"The Balázs? They were always just small-time criminals–"

"But greedy, and they've grown in number since you lived here. They're hyenas wanting to feast on the lion's kill. Just yesterday they torched one of our warehouses destroying a large part of a very valuable shipment. We recovered enough to keep the client satisfied for now, but it reflects badly on us. To say nothing of the lost revenue!"

Kartal interjects: "Was that the weapons for the Armenians?" and when Sándor nods he spits out *baszós [fuckers]*.

"It's a difficult time for the Koczinyi pack to call on the Szémozsas since your pack is in mourning over the loss of Kada but–"

"No, no. Don't worry about that. Gyuri has stepped in already and he assures me he'll do everything he can to return the pack to the way our father ran it. The Szémozsa pack will always stand up for its allies."

"Ah, I'm glad to hear that. Deco Szémozsa made your pack strong and successful. He was a great leader."

Nodding in agreement about my father I comment: "True, but it's no longer my pack."

Sándor waves away that remark. "Gyuri will lift your banishment and both you and Tó will be welcomed home. Congratulations, by the way and how is your lovely bride?"

"She's on her way to you right now. Tó is convinced that Beáta murdered Kada simply because *it's always the husband or wife* and she's determined to launch her own investigation. I'm relying on you, Sándor, to keep her in line."

The older man chuckles. "I've already got my hands full with my own young wife but I'll use my sternest Alpha voice to make them both behave."

Turning serious once again he discusses various options to re-route their next shipment. With input from Kartal they come to a decision.

I listen, but my thoughts are drawn to the very attractive idea of returning to my pack along with my mate. I have to acknowledge that chances were good that I would have the leadership if I'd remained. Despite being the youngest son our father had championed me as his successor.

During my self-imposed exile I realized that neither Beáta nor her parents ever knew that. They just assumed Kada would become our leader because he was the first-born son. Usually it does happen that way... but not always.

Kada might have challenged me but I know I would have won. He was unstable, constantly fighting and quarrelling with everyone, unable to socialize and integrate fully into the pack. But by time Deco died Kada had bullied his way in and banished me, his only real rival.

Gyuri, the second son, willingly stepped back to prioritize his young family. I know that the reputation of the Szémozsa pack suffered under Kada's rule.

During my chosen isolation I learned to repress my longing for the solidarity of pack life. Even though we live as men for most of the time clan members are always very aware of the wolf living inside. My wolf was starved for the camaraderie and that strong sense of belonging pack animals need to thrive.

I was grateful when Grigor showed up on my doorstep demanding to serve his Alpha. The two of us enjoyed our adventures of fighting and fucking our way through gangs and women until our criminal enterprise was as notorious as it was prosperous.

During my time alone l gave in to a vile craving to indulge my dark side. Grigor never shared that bloodlust but he was always ready to help his Alpha dispose of the evidence. He is my closest friend.

When Sándor and Janos travelled from Hungary to the U.S. for that clandestine meeting with me our alliance was still untested. Traditionally each pack governed its own territory, the gangs constantly skirmishing over boundaries. After several generations of independence and warfare we'd all come to the conclusion that uniting the three enterprises would produce a strong empire cornering the market for our criminal endeavors.

There are plenty of illegal income streams to exploit and by staying away from the high revenue/high risk illegal drugs and human trafficking businesses we didn't encroach on the trade of other gangs.

Still, our pact was viewed with distrust which is why our secret meeting was sabotaged by the previously trusted host Milán. He tried to bring us down using Tó in such a way he practically guaranteed she'd be killed horribly. It was Sándor's immense Alpha power that held Janos and I at bay. He was able to keep us from tearing each other's throats out and ripping Tó apart in the process.

The arrival of Tó in my life changed everything. She will love pack life, I realize. My wife has always been willing to explore new experiences, eager to learn, and free of preconceived ideas. She's open and non-judgmental about everything well... everything except her own family. She has extremely limited tolerance for the Royals who first rejected and are now trying to re-claim her. I chuckle at the memory of Prince River's shocked face when Tó told me she wanted him killed.

For many years I kept my longing for my blood clan buried deep down. I'm not an introspective man, always content to hide from thoughts that were just too painful. But now... now I envision pack life not as a leader, I've been away and on my own too long for that responsibility, but as a trusted member with my wife by my side.

Tó will love being part of a community celebrating the good times and banding together to defend against threats like these Balázs are inflicting on the Koczinyi family.

Eventually I come to learn that I'm amazingly wrong in my assessment of my wife – her heart's desire is much simpler than I imagined – but that's because she always keeps her thoughts private while guarding her internal dialog with a bland expression.

Tó is gradually opening up and tentatively trying to trust me. I know she honestly feels a growing love for me, and I hope someday I can feel that way towards her.

Tó's Weak Heat

Tó

Talking about my wedding and then hearing Csilla's memories from her own special day – an exact opposite to our celebration – occupied us for the whole drive back.

I'm sure Grigor and Máté must have been bored to tears. Even my thoughts drifted away while Csilla detailed the difficulties in finding bridesmaid dresses that were acceptable to all six women. Six! with ushers meant twelve in the wedding party plus the bride and groom. All the photos must have needed a wide-angle lens.

Csilla didn't need my attention beyond me saying the occasional *really?* or making *mmm* and *aah* sounds and I soon found my eyes drawn to Máté. He isn't conventionally handsome but he's a very attractive man, intimidating as a protector should be. A very manly specimen with his bulk and his air of suppressed violence. Menacing.

I let myself entertain a fantasy of him and Antal taking me together. I'm imagining being bound by my wrists secured to a ceiling hook. Stretching my body just enough to put tension on my muscles. Completely helpless. I'm naked, of course, and I'm sandwiched between my two fantasy partners. As they embrace me they also reach out to each other and our bodies form an entanglement of hot sweaty flesh. Hands stroking and groping, teeth nipping, their feral growls to each other reverberating through me.

They're both going to invade me at the same time. But my anticipation is heavily weighted with apprehension. Not only will they use me roughly but Antal is a big man and Máté is huge. I'm sure he's got the cock to match his size. They're going to rip me apart if I have to accommodate both of them. Only Antal takes me anally so it will be

Máté pounding into my poor pussy. I'll have to wrap my legs as much around his waist as I can, which will expose my butt-hole for Antal.

My fantasy is turning very heated because I remember being in this exact same position with my Alpha and his Beta. Ah, Grigor! He needs to be part of this erotic scenario, too! Well, they'll just have to lower me to the ground so my mouth can be put to use. Dammit I've imagined myself into a damn good time. I'm their very willing fuck toy with crazed desire from my heat and– oh! oh no! The realization that I'm verging on heat right now knocks me for a loop. No wonder I'm having such vivid erotic daydreams.

Oh God, I'm about to lose my mind. I can't have a heat now when I'm travelling in the wrong direction, heading away from my Alpha. What am I going to do? Even as the panicked thought assails me my gaze can't resist zeroing in on the two big Betas in the front seat of the car.

Csilla has stopped talking and instead is focused on me. As an Alpha herself she can sense my discomfort and possibly my neediness? The two men in the car are equally alert.

Tentatively reaching for my hand Csilla gently asks: "Tó? Tó are you... are you going into heat?"

Suddenly breathless I'm gasping as I say: "I shouldn't be, it's not time. But... but it feels like I'm pre-heat. I-I... I want, I need uh.. I need to build my nest and get out of these horrible clothes, they feel awful!"

It's a struggle to keep from wailing and I know I'm about to lose that battle. Grigor, thank God! has called Antal who I can hear on speaker cursing while his Beta explains. Grigor hands me the phone and I'm settled by the reassuring rumble of my Alpha's soothing words.

"Édesem [my darling] Tó, I'm less than an hour away. I think this must be a false alarm, I'm not sensing my fated mate's call, but I'm on my way. Don't worry *kis lány [little girl]* I'm coming to take care of you."

"Oh hurry *férj [husband]*," I beg, "I need you. I need my Alpha!"

"Grigor!" he commands, "Take care of my Omega until I get there. Keep her comfortable and safe."

"Of course, Alpha," Grigor replies again and again as Antal's voice shouts instructions over the speaker.

Csilla calls out: "We're home now, Antal. I'll make sure Tó has everything she needs until you get here."

He answers her, but I'm too busy yanking my clothes away from my skin and scratching all over to pay further attention to their conversation. I can feel the wetness of my slick pooling and I'm squeezing my thighs to get friction. My temperature's gone way up and my heart is beating like a drum solo.

Máté helps Csilla from the car then comes round to the other side as Grigor is lifting me. I reach for Máté but he steps back when Grigor snarls a warning. My mind battles against my body's disappointment and I remind myself my husband is on his way. Antal will take care of my hurting need.

Csilla hurries us to a small but comfortable room. It's basically just a big round bed heaped with plush velvet throws and silk pillows. A light lemony smell makes the air clean and fresh, and the dim lighting is easy on my dilated eyes. I sigh appreciatively and quickly shed my clothes. Settling in the middle of the mattress with all the soft fabrics swirled around me like a nest I feel the lustful urges taking over.

My skin is hot and sensitive, my pussy aches, and my nipples are taut and tingling. I run my hands all over myself, pinching and rubbing and stroking. I'm fully primed to fuck and my fingers are inadequate.

I need to wait for Antal. I *want* to wait for him. But though I fold my lips and suck them into my mouth I can't stop the little whimpers that escape me. Breathing loudly through my nose fails to calm my racing pulse. My mewling cries turn to groans then gasps of painful longing.

Grigor hears everything as he stands guard outside the door, protecting me from roving Alphas drawn to my scent, but I'm this close to calling him into my nest to fuck me. I hope Csilla can keep Sándor away, that would just be too awkward...

Before I even see or hear him Antal calls out with a vibrating wave and my soul echoes back to him *hurry-hurry-hurry*.

I repeat over and over to myself: *he's close, my Alpha, he's so close, I can't wait, I have to wait.*

Antal bursts through the door in a frenzy. I fling my legs wide apart and his nostrils flare at the aromatic welcome of my sweet slick. My Alpha drops to his knees and yanking my feet over his shoulders immediately dives in to suck and lick and tongue-fuck me. I writhe with sensation but am soon demanding more. I crave the bliss of his cock pounding deep and deeper. Filling me, hurting me, pleasuring me. My orgasms repeat like a rapid-firing weapon while I mindlessly beg and scream.

When I exhaust Antal both Grigor and Kartal appear. They're gentle as they lift me from my husband whose pelvic bone I've been rubbing against hard enough to bruise. Antal groans with tired relief but opens his eyes to meet my gaze with a smile and a nod of permission.

The two Betas are big men and my small body gets swallowed up in their muscled flesh. I don't know which way is up as I'm turned and twisted, holes plundered, strong fingers squeezing and massaging. We're all wet with cum and slick and sweat. Every thing these men do is wonderful, but they can't satisfy me the way my Alpha does.

Now that I've found my fated mate no one else can compare to either his prowess or his peace.

When he's rested enough Antal starts purring and I immediately fling myself into his arms. I don't notice when the others leave. Ravishing my mate I crest on a burning hot wave of chaotic lust and fall quickly, safe in the arms of my protector, my husband.

Csilla

I follow the sound of someone sobbing their heart out and find Tó slumped in the corner of her room. "Sweetheart!" I exclaim as I sink to my knees beside the younger woman.

I can feel my forehead crease into a worried look of concern instead of my usual placid expression as I ask: "Are you in pain? Where does it hurt? Can I help?"

When Tó gives a furious headshake but no verbal answer I can only suspect that she's ashamed of her tears. I draw Tó's head against my breast and rock her gently. Cooing *shushing* noises I gently rub her back.

"Is this a reaction that happens in the aftermath of a heat?" Realizing Tó will need more time to gather herself before answering my questions I give her space and talk about what I'm feeling instead.

"I've never witnessed a heat before and I found it... shocking. You were hurting so badly and Antal, the way he looked when he arrived well, he was frightening and startling with this aura of madness barely held in check. It stirred my Alpha nature which surprised me because it's usually dormant.

Yes, Antal was quite a sight when he came barreling up from our cellar – he took the service road through the back of the property – roaring *where is my wife? where is my Tó?* and everyone quickly got out of his way, merely pointing towards the room you were in.

He was manic in his desperation. He *smelled* you! I could see him sniffing in long draughts of air through his nose and then he made a beeline straight to your door. When he flung it open we could hear you wailing in relief but also in pain and... well *need*, I guess. I mean, that's what it sounded like.

I'm sorry Tó I don't mean to embarrass you..." I've embarrassed myself and trail off uncertainly.

Tó has regained enough of her composure to answer: "It doesn't embarrass me at all. My heats, and the way I act during one, well... these are things I can't control and I'm not going to apologize for that. It would be like being ashamed of my eye color although having met my twin I do feel... not shame but dismay over that connection."

She pauses with her eyes narrowed obviously recalling some bad experience involving her brother that she's tucked deep into her mind.

"Anyhow mostly I'm never embarrassed for the simple reason that I don't remember anything. Obviously the thought of crawling on all fours and begging a man to fuck me would be pretty humiliating if I was in my right mind at the time but I never am.

I don't recall a single thing after the heat is over. That's a good thing, I think, otherwise I'd never be able to rest during my recovery. And the Alphas are all in a confused mental state as well so nobody's pointing fingers.

However this was a *weak heat,* the same as what happened when I got kidnapped from here by the Fehers, and that's why it ended so abruptly. I figure it was brought on by stress. That's why it came early and wasn't so intense–"

"That *wasn't* intense?" I ask feeling my eyes stretch wide. "You mean it's been worse?"

"Oh it's usually much worse than this, but not as bad as when I was on my own. Then I had dry heats which hurt so bad and were utterly terrifying. I didn't start having normal heats until Antal and I had been together for some time. He really took good care of me, always making sure I ate well and got plenty of sleep.

Now I get healthy heats and since we knotted for the first time... oh! that was just a couple of nights ago. Oh! I might be pregnant!" she finishes on a gasp.

"Aww, your first knotting... Yes, there's a chance, but it's not guaranteed. Kada never sired a child, but Gyuri has several. I had trouble falling pregnant but that's generally the case with female Alphas. I've been lucky with my two.

Did you know that Erzsébet is expecting? Janos is ecstatic. They've been married about ten years now and that's a long time to wait."

"Erzsébet doesn't really strike me as the maternal type–"

"Oh she'll be a fierce mama. I think a lot of her prickliness was due to disappointment. She probably imagined she was failing Janos and I suspect there were a number of miscarriages over the years. I don't know, neither of them have ever said anything, but this pregnancy wasn't announced until she was past sixteen weeks. She's become a different person and I'm so happy for them both."

"Antal's tech guy got me online and I've just started researching about packs and heats and all of the stuff I would have learned naturally if my family hadn't abandoned me to die." Her mouth twists with bitterness but she shakes it off. "I only just learned about knotting the other night and I was scared to try it but..." now her thoughts make her smile.

"I already knew that Alphas can't control themselves. That was being used against the three men at the Gentleman's Club, your husband plus Antal and Janos, who were supposed to enter a competitive rutting rage fighting over me. I did everything I could to mask my scent and they exerted all of their power to control their Alpha urges.

Fortunately, your husband is a very strong Alpha. I mean, yeah, we all fucked but that's the thing... they didn't fight over me, they shared. It's almost unheard of with an unclaimed Omega."

"So... it's different now that you're mated to Antal?"

"Oh for sure. It's way better now because he protects me while still seeing to my needs. When I want – need – more than he can provide right away he selects which partners can join in. I figure that's why those lady porn novels with *reverse harems* make sense. We all know that a female can fuck again and again while a male needs time to recover. Having multiple partners takes care of that."

I smooth the puzzled look from my features. I still don't really understand what Tó is describing so I change the subject to ask: "Then why were you crying? You made such a devastating, heartbreaking sound."

"It's because... because I can't bear the thought of losing what I have! Antal is perfect for me, as my lover and protector and shifter. My life was awful. It was just putting one foot forward day after day with no joy or hope or anticipation. I didn't really judge whether or not it was any good it just was what is was. Then Antal entered my world and... he turned everything upside down.

It feels like it happened overnight but I guess it took awhile for me to start actually looking forward to living another day. I enjoy my life, I love being with Antal, and I wish we could have our time together forever but he's been falsely accused and the threat against him is very real."

"Oh Tó that's true but we can fight it and we will be victorious. We *know* Antal didn't commit the murder so they won't be able to prove a negative."

"But with Beáta claiming she saw Antal—"

Interrupting I'm firm when I state: "We'll take care of Beáta, don't worry about that. She'll get what she's got coming."

Tó's lips form a small smile. "So fearsome the way you, the docile mother of young children, speak!" Expressing her gratitude doesn't come easy but her quiet *thank you* is heartfelt.

"I know you love Antal, after all you married him, but I guess I didn't realize your depth of feeling. You are very poised and self-contained. Not cold, but definitely cool. Seeing you like this is both reassuring and disconcerting. I'm glad your heart loves so profoundly but I'm concerned that a break will devastate you."

"And I have to hide it all from Antal. He doesn't like clingy. My air of aloofness gives him challenge he desires," Tó pauses a moment, chuckling before reminding me of what happened the night of her formal introduction to our social circle. "Remember how embarrassed you were to repeat Antal's words, warnings, of what he was going to do to me once we were alone?"

My cheeks burn with a blush as I whisper: "I will *never* be able to forget that! Oh my, it was shocking and... and so erotic." Tó laughs while I just shake my head.

"He reacts to my high-and-mighty attitude like a matador waving his red cape at the bull. I need to hang on to that. He doesn't like weak females."

I purse my lips, thinking over my words before speaking. "Actually... Antal was amazingly gentle and protective with you after your heat ended. I was touched and charmed, frankly, by his behavior. It's a side to him you don't get to see, and I've never seen it before."

Tó sighs with satisfaction, reassured and contented by what I've told her but she tries to lessen her emotion replying: "He is an Alpha, and that means he'll protect anybody."

"Tó, when it comes to you he acts under some sort of *protector imperative* that's really nice to see–"

"And that's what I'm afraid of losing. Antal sprung the marriage on me as a way to fight my brother's claim. I never, ever thought we'd end up married. In fact I would have called it *a marriage made in hell* if anyone suggested it, yet here we are and... and I'm fully invested in him.

Growing up the way I did I never had anything to lose. Oh people could still take from me, from my body in sex or beatings or both if I was caught by strangers while in heat, but they couldn't hurt my heart because I never learned to feel emotion. Now though... well, if they take Antal and lock him away from me I... I believe it will kill me."

I pull Tó back into my arms saying: "Even if, and it won't happen, but even if they do arrest Antal we'll have him freed right away. You aren't going to lose him Tó. You two deserve to be together and Sándor and

I will do everything in our power to keep you together. And Sándor's power is considerable," I add with wifely pride.

We hear men's voices calling and realize Antal is returning for his wife which I find very satisfactory.

Insider's Progress Report

Antal

Réka comes into the room with the waddling walk of the pregnant. She's arm-in-arm with a slightly younger version of herself, her sister Marta Pataky. Marta guides Réka to an overstuffed chair where she sinks down with a sigh of pleasure.

"I don't know how I'm going to get up again, but until then I'm just going to enjoy this comfort," is her greeting to everyone. Her demeanor, as usual, is inquisitive and interested as she looks from one face to another.

Csilla says: "No need to ask if you feel up to this, I just have to look at you. You wear your pregnancy well, Réka Szémozsa."

The two women are close in age and have known each other for years. Réka chortles her answer: "I've had enough practice, that's for sure! Anyhow, everyone this is my baby sister Marta who works at the police station and has some sort of flirtation going on with István Kovács, one of the detectives on your case Antal, so she's got the insider scoop."

"István is just a friend," protests Marta but her blush indicates she has romantic feelings for the man. "Some of what I'm going to tell you is what he told me, other stuff I overheard or read in a report, and the rest I pieced together from the way my coworkers are acting—"

"Wait, before she gets started I can see you've got some food ready for us Csilla, and I'm starving. Can Gyuri fix me a plate? otherwise I won't be able to concentrate."

Csilla jumps up motioning Gyuri to stay seated while she puts together a meal for Réka. "Everyone helps yourselves, we might as well eat and get comfortable," she announces but no one else is interested in food right now.

"So it's just me being piggy? Well, I can't help it. I'm in heat and I'm hungry all the time."

"Heat makes you hungry? and you still get heats when you're pregnant?" Tó doesn't bother to hide her surprise.

"When you're pregnant it's called a *warm heat*, it's restful. I just feel lazy and sleepy and ravenously hungry, but only for food. I mean, pregnancy hormones always heighten the libido but this kind of heat is easy. Remember Csilla? oh, no of course you wouldn't.

Anyhow I've got my food so I won't interrupt any more while Marta tells her story."

Marta smiles at her sister and begins.

"The first thing István and his partner, Anikó Varga, did was demand their boss *keep that old fool Garai out of the investigation*. Károly Horváth is a very good boss and a good leader so of course he reprimanded them for calling Senior Inspector Garai *an old fool*, but then he went on to assure them that he'd personally see the man was sidelined.

Now I'm not going to bother you with *who said what* and *how so-and-so responded*, the crux of the matter is I'm positive they suspect the widow is the killer. Their second choice is that she's very much involved with the killer, like maybe he's a lover? Regardless of whether she acted alone or not, the thing that was made crystal clear is her statement doesn't line up with the facts."

"Ahhh," says Gyuri with satisfaction. "That's good to hear. Réka? You've said from the start you suspect Beáta."

Tó leans forward with interest. "Réka, why do you feel that way?"

"Well... apologies up-front for sounding catty but I can't stand the woman. We always tried to avoid seeing Kada and Beáta but there are social obligations that, as a family and pack members, we're committed to attend.

Honestly she's just so nasty with her spiteful gossip plus all the sniping and backbiting at her husband. If looks could kill they'd have slain each other years ago!"

"Hey Sis, don't hold back!" giggles Marta.

"Tó suspects Beáta too," I chime in, "but only because she's jealous of our past history."

Tó's look of outrage is comical and everyone has a chuckle. "I think you're projecting, brother," replies Gyuri dryly. "If anyone is jealously possessive it's you. Everyone can see how you scowl at any man who comes near your wife."

Refusing to respond to that comment I purse my lips while Tó smirks.

"My husband is correct when he says I also suspect Beáta. Not based on what I know, because I've never met the woman, but just playing the odds. Crimes committed in the home, *domestics* as they're called in the U.S., are almost always down to the spouse. Next, is a kid or a parent, maybe a relative or close family friend, a rival or an enemy, and then last of all comes a stranger."

Tó's matter-of-fact delivery of this chilling hierarchy of suspects leaves everyone a bit unsettled. She senses this and turns to me with a questioning look.

I lift her onto my lap and holding her close say: "Everyone is thinking how well-suited we are, my cold-hearted wife."

Tó lightly punches my arm claiming: "I'm not cold-hearted... I'm heartless, there's a difference."

Csilla can be heard murmuring *made for each other.*

"Another reason they are looking at the widow is what they call *negative evidence*," continues Marta. We all give her an inquiring look except Tó, our true crime expert, who nods knowingly.

"It means there's nothing to link Antal to the crime scene. Their neighborhood is closed in, like a cul-de-sac, so anyone coming in or out has to use the one and only roadway. There's a camera at the entrance and no car carrying Antal shows up that evening.

It isn't a gated community so sure, anyone can gain access on foot through backyards, but lately there's been a wave of vandalism to the cars parked outside so a number of people have their dashcams working all night. They suspect teenagers who actually live there with their parents. It's going to be a hell of a mess to sort out once they do catch someone..." she pauses to consider concerns voiced in the police station.

"Anyhow, the point is no one was recorded walking around that night and it sounds like it would be impossible not to be spotted. If the backdoor had been broken into, or if a window in the back had been smashed, then maybe someone could enter Kada's house unseen but that isn't the case."

"This is proof!" exclaims Réka, but Marta shakes her head explaining: "It's evidence that the available technology didn't capture Antal on film but it's not concrete proof that he was never there."

"And that's why trials have juries, because humans can understand the value of negative evidence even if the *strict letter of the law* can't," Tó happily puts in.

The rest of the company make disappointed noises and I'm sure my smile is twisted when I explain to my wife that we don't have jury trials in this country. Her look of dismay is so exaggerated it would be comical under different circumstances.

To soothe her I add: "But the accused is still *innocent until proven guilty* putting the burden of proof on the prosecution."

"The other news isn't so good, though. Someone, and I think we all know who, has demanded you, Antal, be extradited from the United States. They have no idea that you're already here."

"Can they do that? I mean, does America allow it?"

Sándor steps in declaring with authority: "Yes, absolutely. I was involved in the process as a third party in a case so I learned something about it. This was, hmmm, about twenty or twenty-five years ago, soon after an extradition treaty was signed between our governments."

"Closer to thirty years, sir," states Marta. She pulls some papers from her purse and continues: "I made some notes because it's all new to me. They began negotiating in 1994 and the treaty was finalized in 1997. Here's what's required:

A copy of the warrant or order of arrest issued by a judge or other competent authority, and a copy of the indictment or other document specifying the charges against the person whose extradition is sought.

There are specific rules for something called a *provisional arrest* and for *seizure of property* but the first thing they have to do is lay charges and issue an arrest warrant and the department is not willing to go that far, not now at least."

"That doesn't mean they won't bring you in for questioning if they discover you're here, Antal," cautions Sándor. "*A Magyar Koztarsasag*

Kormanya [the Government of the Republic of Hungary] won't issue a warrant for extradition, but I think it's likely that the National Police will arrest you on suspicion if they find you."

I nod in agreement stating I can hide back at the village. "I'll make Kartal's home my base, it's so well-hidden, and that way none of you will be compromised."

"No, you will stay with us!" declares Gyuri with Réka insisting *yes, come home.*

"I will formally lift your banishment and welcome you back into the Szémozsa pack. Just let them try to arrest you from my home!"

Sitting on my knee puts Tó close enough to catch the brief flicker of emotion I feel cross my face. To everyone else my expression remains impassive as I gravely thank Gyuri and Réka but remain firm about waiting until my name is cleared first.

"Now, if Beáta's statement is muddled about times everyone else's have to be perfectly clear, right? So, I saw you and Kada when you two came to the Castle after Tó was kidnapped–"

"We can't mention that!"

"Well, Beáta will tell the police that Kada and I were recently in touch so I have to say something."

"Okay, how about this: I'll say that I brought Kada to meet with you to discuss a reconciliation with the pack and that I'm *cautiously optimistic.* I'll make it clear we all left on friendly-ish terms."

"We had a few dozen people at the soiree so there's no disputing where you were the day Kada was killed. The police will accept Sándor's word of what time he and I drove you to the airfield for your flight home that night. I suppose you could have flown some distance then turned around but there would be records of that with Air Traffic Control," says Csilla.

"Plenty of people saw Kada and Beáta leaving our home. He was so rude that they'll remember for sure and it supports our story. Antal I really don't think you have anything to worry about."

The room is silent for a minute while everyone thinks about the *he said, she said* scenario of Beáta's word against mine but I have corroboration. And from credible sources.

"I think you're right, Csilla but I want more this time. I don't want my name connected to the slightest suspicion of guilt. I may be a criminal but I don't want people wondering if I got away with murdering my brother.

I want the true killer found not to punish, I hated Kada and couldn't care less that he's dead, but to clear me once and for all."

Turning to look at Gyuri I add: "I want to reconnect with my pack, very much! but not with any kind of threat hanging over me. It would taint my return."

Tó climbs off my lap and looking into the faces of everyone gathered announces: "You heard him, now let's get to work!"

Council of War

Antal

Tó led our *council of war* where we decided someone needs to get close to Beáta so we can find out what she's up to. Imre is the logical choice to help although I'm still angry at him for abusing Tó last week.

As teenagers in school we were all close friends although it was Stefan who Beáta had a major crush on back then. It didn't take long for Stefan's sexual identity to resolve itself which gave me an opportunity with her. Imre remained ambiguous, and I'm sure he's still capable of flattering her with conviction.

I put my phone on speaker and give him a call. He sounds happy to hear from me and eager to talk. "Antal! I'm glad you called, I didn't like the way we left things and then you went back home–"

"I'm not at home now, I'm back here in Hungary," I explain.

He hurries to ask: "Can we meet?"

"Ah no, I'm actually traveling under the radar so to speak. Listen, did you hear that my brother Kada was killed?"

"I did and oh! um, sorry for your loss?" his voice trails off uncertainly.

"Yeah no, fuck that! As you can imagine I'm glad he's dead. No, the thing is Beáta accused me of killing him. She claims she's an eyewitness!"

"Wait, what? If she says she saw you kill him but you didn't kill him them she must have done it, right?"

"Unless there was another man there, someone my size? with my coloring? I suppose it's possible she believes her story. Anyhow, I'm sure I was already flying over the Atlantic when he died but there's some discrepancy about the time of death. Because she's lying Beáta's story is full of holes, we just have to prove it. Anyhow, are you still in touch with her at all?"

"Not really. She and Kada didn't socialize much, at least not as a couple so I don't see much of her but we're still friendly, I guess."

"So it won't seem weird for you to pay her a condolence call?"

"No, not at all. I'll phone her up and ask whatever you like–"

"Actually can you do it in-person? You know how good she lies but her body always used to betray her with little tells. You'll be able to catch her out and probe, put her on the spot."

Imre pauses to think before replying: "Yeah sure, I think I'll enjoy doing that. I can't believe she's accusing you, though. What's that all about? Is she jealous or something?"

"No, but if she's the killer then she figured I was a convenient scapegoat because of past history and the coincidence of Kada being killed just as I returned after all these years. She didn't realize we were heading back home right away."

"I see. But you know I wouldn't put it past her to be vengeful, spiteful, whatever you want to call it. She was never a nice person and she hasn't improved with age, neither of them did. But anyways, what exactly do you want me to find out?"

"Get her to tell you the whole story and then we'll figure out the weak spots."

"To what end, exactly?"

"What do you mean?"

"Well, are you going to kill Beáta this time?"

His words make me see red and I almost end the call before quietly asking: "Imre what do you mean *this time*?"

He hears the anger in my voice and stammers a bit before clearing his throat in a fake cough saying: "Well... that was you who assaulted her back then, right?"

"No of course it wasn't!" I retort, louder than I meant. "I didn't have to rape Beáta, we were lovers, and I would never have beaten her."

"But... she broke up with you, didn't she?"

"Yeah, she did but, as soon as she mentioned Kada I realized exactly what happened. He went after her simply because she was mine, you know what he was like, and once she got involved with him it killed any interest I had in her. I had no reason to punish her with violence, if I'd cared enough I would have gone after him. No we're all convinced, my family that is, that Kada was the one who attacked her."

"And then blamed you... what a bastard! and now it's the same story all over again so... oh! I'm sure Beáta must have killed Kada!"

"Well, I'm not 100 percent certain but my wife is convinced."

"Your... you married Tó?"

"Well of course I did, she's my fated mate and–"

"She is? If Tó's your fated mate... does that mean you've finally–"

"It means I've knotted her, yes."

"Oh man, well congrats for sure."

"In fact, we should be on our honeymoon right now but instead I'm hiding out while she's staying with the Koczinyis."

"Oh I see, no actually I don't, that's... um–"

Tó, ever irrepressible, speaks up to say *thanks, Imre*. I shake my head at her and she grins back at me. Returning to the call I ask Imre to see Beáta as soon as he can and to let us know the results. He promises to see her right away, deciding it's best to just drop in instead of phoning ahead of time.

"That sounds great, thanks. If you can't get hold of me call Gyuri, okay?"

"Sure, will do Antal and... I'm glad you called, bro. I'll take care of this for sure."

I don't want to put Sándor in an awkward position with the authorities so when Kartal suggests we stay here tonight and make an early start in the morning I say no. His village isn't far and traveling back and forth isn't a problem. I turn to Tó and her eyes sparkle as she accurately reads my look.

"I'm going to go back with my husband. At least for tonight. All this talk of honeymooning, well..." Everyone smiles indulgently at my pretty bride.

"Am I driving you or do you want to take the car?" asks Kartal. I tell him I'll drive the two of us and ask what landmark to look for in order to find the turnoff to his village.

"Oh it's easy at night! There's luminous green paint on a small cairn of rocks marking the lane on the right-hand side of the road. There are no lights out there so drive slowly in case some villager's animals have drifted on to the pathway. Then keep going until you get to my place, there's a lantern always lit at the end of my driveway."

I gather up Tó who will spend ages saying goodbye unless I intervene and we head out to the car. Once we're on the road she undoes her seat-belt, buckling it to itself so the alarm doesn't beep, and slides over for a cuddle saying she likes the bench seat in this car.

"If we get a ticket for no seat-belt you pay the fine," I tell her.

"Oh they'll be too busy arresting you to worry about me," she teases.

"No seat-belt *and* with a disrespectful mouth... remind me to punish you when we get back."

"Yeah, right. As if you need reminding... Oooh!" she squeals as I find a nipple and tweak it hard.

"That's true but it's such a turn-on to make you ask for your punishment, to make you beg for it."

Slipping her little hand over my thigh and right into my crotch she fingers my cock like she's playing the piano. "Oh I'll always beg to be punished with this big weapon of yours."

"Behave while I'm driving wife or we'll end up in the ditch and you'll get injured since you don't have your seat-belt on."

"How come the only time you and I ever go driving together, just the two of us, is when we're in Hungary?"

"I don't know... I guess we don't often go anywhere back home, and Grigor always drives when we do. Although I did do some of the driving the first time I brought you to my house. In the limo, remember?"

Her wicked smile tells me that she sure does remember. Janos' driver was an older man but by God he had staying power. I needed a break from my Omega's insatiable heat so I switched places with the chauffeur who had enough stamina to wear Tó out. She came three times, maybe four, while he steadily pumped away at her.

I know because I watched through the rearview mirror. Once my little brat realized I could see her she put on quite a show for me. He had her in several positions and by time he finished she was tapped out: satisfied and sleepy. I chuckled then and the memory amuses me all over again now.

"Tó, I really like you."

"Good to know, you did marry me after all."

No, I mean I like this... you and me, the way we are now."

"Shy with embarrassment Tó replies: "That's just your dick talking–"

I interrupt her to say: "No, not at all. It's just when you're in heat you are wild, demanding, voracious and it makes me savage and dominant and it's fantastic but it's not you."

"I can assure you it is me," she exclaims.

"No, I mean you-you, *you're* not there."

"Okay now you've totally lost me–"

Frustrated I turn to look straight at her while struggling to find the words.

"Tell me in Hungarian and what I don't understand we'll figure out," she suggests.

So that's what I do, explaining that when she's in heat the sex is phenomenal but she's not Tó, she's not my wife, she's my Omega, my fated mate. But now I see the real woman, just Tó, and I not only love her and lust after her but I like her. A lot.

I finish up by saying: "I'm so glad I found you."

I'm sure she understood most of that because her eyes are shining and her grin is so wide her cheeks must hurt. She doesn't speak, just places her head on my chest with a contented sigh. I can steer one-handed so I slip my arm around her shoulders and pull her close.

We both spot the green stones saying *there!* at the same time. Tó shouts *snap!* and I have no idea why, but I don't get a chance to ask because the utter blackness means I need all my concentration to drive safely.

Under Attack

Antal

Taking Tó by the hand I lead her into the bedroom where I begin undressing. Tó said that watching me unbutton my shirt is always a pleasure so I go slow. Her eyes are glued to my body and as my hard-muscled torso, decorated with all my colorful tats, comes into view she licks her lips. I notice but choose to ignore the gesture and continue to strip, keeping my face expressionless.

"Feleség [wife], you and I are going for a run. If we're going to be spending time with my pack you're going to need more stamina which means we have to practice, practice, practice."

"Mmm, sounds like fun, *férj [husband]*," she replies with a smile, her eyes still focused on my almost-naked body.

Tilting up Tó's chin I force her to meet my eyes. My gaze promises a threat that makes her shiver in fearful anticipation.

Keeping my voice barely above a whisper I warn: "I'll have fun but you? not so much. I'm going to run you ragged and when you collapse, utterly exhausted, I'm going to ride your worn-out body hard. You'll be flopping around like a rag-doll, skewered by my cock, while I rut you into the dirt. If you want any kind of a head start you better shift now and *run*!"

Tó squeals and quickly shucks her clothes. In the next second there's a flash of silver but then it's gone as her lithe wolf races away. I take the time to stretch as a warm-up before I too shift into my animal form. I let a happy growl rumble in my chest as I trot towards the forest. I'm not worried about Tó managing to escape me because I've got Kartal and Grigor flanking her left and right.

100

Once Tó realizes it's not just her and me out in the woods she'll realize her evasive actions of sharp turns and veering off sideways will only tire her faster. She'll send out a signal of desperation as she forces a burst of speed and that's when I'll go from stalker mode to attack mode.

The fear in Tó's scent will be maddening, spurring me on. My beast will break free and Tó will become my prey.

Already I'm subconsciously filling my lungs with deep breaths so I can increase my speed while maintaining my stamina. It feels so good, so fucking good to be free and running and chasing and hunting again. I don't even try to contain the howl that breaks loose and mine is immediately echoed back by both of the Betas.

I can feel that my mate is on the edge of panic, knowing the males are closing in and knowing what will happen when she's caught.

Tó

My wolf mind registers *danger!* when I hear racing bodies crashing through the woods on either side of me. I know my Alpha is behind, and rapidly closing in, so it must be his Betas herding me at his command. There's enough of my human self's awareness left inside to complain *no fair!* but this primal hunt has nothing to do with fairness. I excel in making acute turns and cornering, but my zigzagging pattern has only brought me closer to the wolves running interference.

My agility is no match against my Alpha's powerful drive forward and I'm soon driven into the same clearing again. This time the sky is cloudy so only a shimmering of moonlight highlights the silver in my fur. My breath is coming in rasping pants from equal parts exertion and exhaustion.

When my Alpha latches onto his mate's neck my front legs splay as he drives me down to the ground. The Betas snuffle and whine with excitement. The big gray wolf blends so well with the darkness he's only a shadowy form and hard to track. But the Betas can hear him snap his jaw when he snarls at them to *back off*. The victor is demonstrating his unwillingness to share his catch this time.

With their tails drooping down the other two wolves head out of the clearing but soon the sound of them racing each other echoes back.

The slender she-wolf is compelled to submit to her fated mate and she's ravished and rutted in rapturous pain. I'm greedy for my pleasure.

Our coupling is electrifying and intense. When Antal commands me to shift I remain trapped under his large furry body and he nips at my pale flesh for a minute or two before he turns back. I gasp because moving my arm hurts and I see his claws left a bloody gash. Antal laps up the blood from the shallow wound and I'm so thankful he didn't smell it while he was still in animal form.

Turning on to my back I complain to my husband: "You didn't catch me, you cornered me. Three against one isn't fair!"

Antal's grin is ferocious and frightening. His shining eyes travel all over my naked body, and I shiver under his hungry gaze. Grabbing me behind my knees Antal lifts my pelvis up and thrusts deeply inside me.

I cry out at the roughness of the assault but Antal's pelvic bone hits against my clit just right and that little bundle of nerves lights up. I squirm to rub harder and soon that white-hot sensation is burning through my core. My scream of ecstasy sounds far off to me but it startles an owl into flight, the draft from its huge wingspan fanning down on us. We are private, here in the clearing, but never truly alone.

Antal's human groan is almost as loud as his wolf's howl – it's certainly as wild. He keeps pounding at me until I'm ready to cum with him. In a sweaty frenzy we climax then collapse, chests heaving. Antal's mouth presses down hard on my lips and we fill our lungs with each other's heaving exhalations.

After a while Antal flops over onto his back and the two of us lie side-by-side. We're both silent as we stare up through the opening above the ring of trees. Clouds move quickly opening up a glimpse of starry skies before graying over again. The wind has picked up as well. It's a cold night but the chase and our passion keep our bodies warm enough.

"I never once said I would treat you fairly, Tó. I won't. I always want to win which means I always want you to lose. To lose to me."

"Just because that's what you want doesn't mean that's what you should get, Antal."

He turns his head to give me a puzzled frown saying: "Of course it does! I am your Alpha so you will grant me my desires. I rule you."

I prop myself up on one elbow and looking down at my husband lying recumbent say: "When I submit it's because I choose to do so. I act out of my desire and my hunger, that's all. This is my version of love."

Antal pulls me to lie on top of his body and spanking my ass twice says: "Defiant girl!"

I squeal at the sting before murmuring: "Make-belief Master."

Quickly, before Antal can react to that insult I shift back into my wolf and flee the clearing. I have enough of a head-start that Antal's commanding wave is too weak to knock me to my knees. He gives bloodcurdling howls as he crashes through the undergrowth and once again my libido heats up at my mate's pursuit. The age-old song between an Alpha and his Omega.

The big wolf quickly catches up but now that it's *the dark before the dawn* he sends the command *home* and the two of us run back to Kartal's place at an easy lope.

Whatever plans we'd made for the bedroom have to be shelved when we're greeted by serious, anxious faces.

I hurry to our room to shift and get dressed but Antal doesn't waste time. Back in his naked human form he demands to know what's going on as he heads towards his clothing.

Antal

Grigor speaks first: "The Balázs pack has attacked the Castle and the Koczinyis need our help."

"A sneak attack when everyone is sleeping! Women and children, old and sick, those *kutyas [dogs]* don't care. They need to be put down. We must go to my Alpha's aid right now," exclaims Kartal, the worry evident in his voice.

I grab up the clothes I left on the bed and Tó runs to fetch my boots from the closet. I tell her to stay safe with the women. "Keep out of trouble, *szerelmem [my love]*."

I press a bruising kiss on her mouth before leaving with Grigor, an impatient Kartal fidgeting behind the wheel of the car. *En route* at a furious pace Grigor relates what little they know.

"The Koczinyis are defending their front, your brother has brought the Szémozsa pack in through the back, and by time Janos arrives with his men we hope to have the *baszós [fuckers]* neatly trapped."

I nod, saying *good, good*. The three united packs are allied through marriages and businesses and always support each other. After a moment's thought I say: "I don't understand why the Balázs are

104

attacking, I mean what is their Alpha thinking? His pack isn't strong enough on its own and he has no allies."

"He must think we've been weakened after our battle with the Fehers, and that the Szémozsa pack is leaderless now that Kada is gone."

"But Gyuri is a good fighter, as vicious as he needs to be, he always has been—"

"But no one knows that," interrupts Kartal. "Kada always acted like nobody else did anything and he had to do it all himself. But thank God Gyuri is a very good friend to my Alpha and his pack is ready to fight for us."

He ends on a growl which Grigor and I join in on with feral anticipation. We're all ready and eager to taste the blood of our enemies.

Our wish is fulfilled.

Arriving through the back road on to the Castle grounds for the second time we follow the route Gyuri took. In the faint light of early morn the three of us are met with a hellish scene of violence awash with blood.

The reeking stench of gore compels our human selves to shift so the battle is between savage beasts. No wolf is a match against even the weakest human with a gun, but a fighting wolf pack is a vicious and deadly force.

The air is filled with screams, howls, and snarling. With grim delight I shift and bound straight into the melee, closely followed by my companions. I love warring against enemy fighters.

Each of us battle ferociously, reveling in bloodlust and vengeance. Snapping jaws, ripping flesh, growling and yipping sounds echo through the service yard, the graveled surface soaking up a river of blood.

Sándor sends out a strong Alpha command to *kill the intruders!* and the attackers are massacred by the sheer force of the enraged defenders joined by their many allies.

The hair around my jaws is caked with blood and drool. I sink my teeth into flesh and shake it furiously as foamy drops fly outwards. The smell, the taste, the sounds combine to ramp up the ferocity of my brutal attack.

I am ruthless, barbarous, and hungry for more. It's been so long – too long – since I've fulfilled myself by playing my part in a part of a ravaging pack. War and death have brought me back to life with lusty vitality, satisfying my penchant for violence.

The bulk of the Balázs pack attacked from the rear and were met by the Koczinyi pack with a crushing rearguard offensive from the Szémozsas. Since the pack isn't large their leader could only afford to send a small number for the frontal assault.

The fire they started there was doused before it could cause any serious damage, and the humans who lay dead never had a chance to fire the weapons that lie scattered around. All the female Alphas of the Koczinyi clan are well-trained in defensive tactics so they easily repelled the invaders.

The Balázs pack is fueled by greed and aggression, not honor or fealty. Sensing their defeat a group breaks away to flee through the woods but the Erdős pack led by Janos is waiting to cut down any escapees.

When Kada ruled the Szémozsas there was a lack of cohesiveness and loyalty. He never earned the respect and love of his pack-mates but they have rally as a unified force under Gyuri's leadership. The honor of winning is shared equally. Victory has the pack males roused and the she-wolves ready for mating. I howl long and loud wishing Tó was close enough to hear me coming for her.

"Kartal, you have work to do with your Alpha and I know how to get to your home now so I'll take your car and fetch Tó–"

"Alpha, I will drive you," interrupts Grigor, but I stop him knowing the Koczinyis urgently need everyone available to help with repairs and reinforcement of the Castle.

Return of the Warrior

Antal

Driving down the E60 to Kartal's village I realize this is the first time in at least a week that I've been completely alone. Alone and reeking from the slime of war. Navigating the highway is so straightforward it's easy to let my concentration drift. My mind is crowded with so many different thoughts.

Even though I was an excellent student, intelligent and well-read, I never completed my education. Like my wife I was forced to flee for my very survival, and like Tó I developed vital street skills.

I'm a fighter. I'm violent and I'm strong. But underneath my tough, brutal exterior I have a good brain and a logical reasoning mind. I'm not much given to introspection, I'm more inclined to just... be. I accept myself the way I am and that's all there is to it. But then Tó came into my life with all the power of an underfed kitten yet she disrupted something deep inside.

I've changed.

She obediently gives me her body, compliant as a malleable doll, but I know she withholds her thoughts and emotions. Her gorgeous eyes are shuttered to my gaze. I've used pain to reach her innermost self but she never breaks. It was a surprise to realize that I don't want to break her, although I still inflict pain and relish her reactions. I want everything from her but most of all I need her to share her private self willingly.

Women have always been attracted to my looks, my macho swagger, and what Tó calls my *Alphaholeness* which is simply my cruel nature. I've taken and then discarded without consideration, guilt, remorse... any of those feelings. I've been a cold, dangerous, humorless man.

Until Tó... a *kis nyuszi [little bunny]* who showed her bravery when I sent her out of the Gentlemen's Club into a possible ambush with nothing more than a kiss. I changed her name from the English *Lake* to the Hungarian *Tó* declaring her my *kis lány, kis farkas-lány (little girl, little wolf-girl).*

My Tó. I never considered if taking her with me when I left was the right or wrong thing to do, it just felt necessary.

With proper care that skinny little girl has grown into a healthy young woman who constantly provokes me. She wants my smiles thinking a mellow mood will chase away my bloodthirsty demons and to an extent it does. I feel my harsh resolve weakening in my urge to please her. I learned to school my expression years ago and easily maintain an impassive mien but Tó... she warms me inside.

As I crawl through the bumpy village lane every person I pass stops to wave. It's very friendly and yet if Kartal hadn't vouched for us we'd have been met with the stony gazes and cold shouldering the inhabitants show outsiders.

Someone must have phoned to say I'm on my way because Tó's waiting outside where the driveway meets the road. She starts waving as soon as she sees the car. Pulling up I park and barely get the door open before she's flinging her arms round my neck joyously exclaiming *you're home! you're safe! I missed you!*

When I shifted back into human form after the battle I had to put my clothes back on over my bloody, stinking flesh. In my hurry to get home I spared no time to clean up. Tó couldn't care less, she isn't repelled by the sight or the smell.

I swing my legs out from under the steering wheel so I have room to lift her onto my lap. I give her a closed-mouth kiss refusing to open up even though she licks my lips and makes the most endearing mewling whimpers. Pulling back I hold her in place with my fingers wrapped around her chin.

Staring into her eyes I admonish: "Of course I'm safe. You never need to worry about me *feleség [wife]* I am a *harcos [warrior]*, and a *jó vadászgép [good fighter]*."

"Of course, *édesem férj [my darling husband]*. Now kiss me properly," she says batting her eyelashes at me. Still keeping a firm grip on her chin I cover her mouth with my own and pressing hard I let my passion flow. I strive to communicate so much with this kiss and I feel Tó's body soften until she's boneless in my arms.

Breaking free I keep my lips just a hairsbreadth away as I whisper endearments: "*Csinos kislány [pretty girl]*, *édes baba [sweet baby]*, *szeretlek, szivem [I love you, my heart]*."

I hug her tightly and stepping out of the car spin around with Tó laughing in my arms. Looking up in wonder she cries: "Antal do you see that? the trees are dancing!"

"Yeah it's windy out, I even felt on the road."

"No, I mean look at those trees, it's exactly like they're dancing. The tops are swaying and the branches are all moving up and down like arms and legs. It just like they're moving to music."

I smile at the childlike delight in my bride's voice. The pine trees of the forest do shift and their branches do flutter. Taking a longer look I agree that one could imagine the trees are responding to a tune on a frequency too high for humans to hear. The wind is strong with powerful gusts. It's the type of weather that calls to our wolf nature.

"Strip, *feleség [wife]* and let's have a daylight run with the wind."

Tó doesn't hesitate, flinging off her clothes and shifting into her wolf form. She bounds away and my big gray wolf catches her up but doesn't overtake her. We run side by side, aided by the gusts at our backs.

Racing for pleasure is a new experience for Tó. Previously she only shifted in defense, to run or fight. She'd learned never to admit to humans that she was dual-natured. That truth was always met with envy, fear, disgust, or challenge. Here in the protective seclusion of Kartal's village she can freely and safely indulge in the joy of running with her fated mate.

I'm stretching my limbs with satisfaction. It's a moment when I regret spending so much of my time as a biped instead of exhilarating in the power of my wolf form. I resolve that when Tó and I return to America we'll make opportunities to run. *If we return*, I think. *Maybe we should think very seriously about staying here and living with the pack.* I look over at Tó and am pleased to see how she races in an adrenaline rush then flops down to roll around in fragrant clover. She frolics and yips joyously and it's delightful to see.

As a wolf I can easily rip out a throat, gnaw through a limb, claw a body savagely, and kill, yet I don't feel any dark urges or twisted desires. I only get the sadistic bloodthirst to harm and maim and torture when I'm human. *Maybe I only get monstrous when my wolf's needs have been thwarted for too long?* Although I'm not the kind of man to spend time on self-reflection I do plan to put this theory to the test.

Knotting my mate was the greatest experience of my life, far surpassing the black impulses that used to lead me to gory killing. I'm determined to spend more time, maybe even equal time, enjoying both aspects of my nature. It's not that I hate my inner demons. but I sometimes worry about going too far and hurting Tó too much.

Grinning at my mate I share in her happiness. My Alpha wave is uplifting and joyous.

After a run of half-an-hour or so we head back to Kartal's home. Our clothes are exactly where we left them but before we can shift and dress three she-wolves, a blonde and two brunettes, hurry out to herd us behind the house.

Curious, we abandon our clothes and follow Kartal's servants through a vegetable garden and a small orchard before arriving at a natural thermal spring.

The females shift to their human forms and their lovely nude bodies shimmer in the steam rising from the water. Tó is quick to join them and I sit on my haunches content to watch the young women play.

Floating, splashing, and ducking each other their excited giggles turn to infectious laughter. Colors fade in the dusk but their wet skin shines and sparkling droplets swing out from their hair as they jump and spin.

At a chorus of *join us, Antal!* I shift and stretch to my full height. My cock grows hard at the frank approval I see in their admiring glances. All the stresses and tensions of the day dissipate in the pool of hot water, along with the bloody residue of the battle.

As I float the girls encircle me, holding hands, and chanting some nursery rhyme or lullaby, I don't know what it is, but their high voices are gently pretty.

Breaking free Tó swims into my arms and I steer us to the water's edge and turning trap her between me and the bank. As I kiss my wife I can feel the others drawing close. Soft skin brushes against my back, butt, and legs. Small hands reach out to caress my shoulders and Tó's arms.

Soon the two of us are wrapped in a sensual warm wet embrace. Inquisitive fingers stroke my cock while another female's hand cups my balls. Tó's arms are around my neck and thinking of these young strangers touching me makes me grow even harder. Tó winks letting me know she's aware of what's going on under the water. She presses her body closer until I can feel her hard little nipples against my chest.

Gentle fingers stroke me from head to toe and I see hands massaging Tó's body as well. The females aren't trying to intrude but instead are honoring the union of two fated mates. Each of them hopes to someday meet her own. Meanwhile they're happy to provide some sensuous stimulation to us.

Lost in our kiss I don't notice when the girls leave us, but when I realize we're alone I spread Tó's legs and push my length deep inside. The tender walls of her passage grip me tightly as I let the motion of the water rock us together. I want this moment to last but a flashback to the death and destruction of today's fighting heats my blood and I revel in being alive and triumphant.

I give my wife a good hard victory fuck, and she welcomes every thrust from her warrior with a squeeze, a hug, from her sweet cunt.

I can't get enough of her slippery shiny body. She turns easily in the water and I lift her upper half onto the bank allowing her to hold on while I drive in deep. Standing, I hook her knees over my elbows and hold her like a wheelbarrow, spreading her wide. Fuck me her snatch is so tight and so hot, all for me.

"Rub yourself," I order and Tó quickly complies.

Rapid fingers work at her sensitive clit and soon her hips are bucking as she gets closer, closer, closer. I heave hard and poor Tó gets shoved facedown into the ground just as her orgasm hits and I can't hold back a second longer. In a frenzy of thrusts I empty streams of cum inside Tó giving a long drawn-out groan of *wiiiiiiiife* before collapsing onto her back.

I only rest for seconds before lifting my weight off her. Tó lazily rolls around to face me and that's when I see she's dirt-stained from forehead to belly with streaks of blood from banging her nose. Completely unaware of how she looks my girl smiles at me and I growl *mine, mine, mine* before dragging her back into pool of the hot spring to rinse the blood and dirt away.

We're naked and sated and we take our time walking back to the house. The sun died in an explosion of fiery oranges and reds before fully setting. The darkness drops down suddenly and I can't see Tó. Just as I reach out for her she reaches for me and I hold her little hand in mine. We can see the welcoming lights of Kartal's place and head that way.

Detouring down the driveway I find the car and Tó gathers up our clothes. I feel for the hard bulge of the keys and click the fob to lock the car. Probably not necessary way out here but it's not my car so I'm not taking any chances.

With our backs to the glowing windows of the house we can see the twinkle of stars appearing in the night sky. Tó's skin gleams in the cold light of the rising moon and I push her against the car while I run my hands up and down her smooth body. Her eyes glint and I bend to take possession of her mouth. Tó's thin lips are so delicate between my teeth, and her tongue darts like a tiny fish in and out of my mouth. My fingers tangle in the silk of her hair as I cradle her head. Her hands snake around my neck and her fingers massage behind my ears. Time stands still when we're fused together this way.

The spell is broken when Duna calls to us to come indoors. I'm reluctant to end our kiss but when we break apart I immediately feel the chill of the night air. Tó sashays towards the house until I hurry her up with a smack to her butt. She squeals and jogs ahead.

Duna, Kinga, and Ilka are all in the doorway waiting. The girls excitedly explain that Kartal has called and wants everyone to come to the Castle in the morning. We're needed to help clean up and repair and then we'll all celebrate the victory with a night of feasting, drinking, and dancing.

An Engraved Invitation

Early the next morning me and Kartal's three women squeeze into the car while Antal drives us to the Castle. I'm glad I don't have to squish into the back because my lady-parts are achingly sore after last night's marathon sex session.

The battle with the Balázs pack aroused Antal's bloodlust and whet his appetite for power and violence. After our interlude of gentle play in the hot spring he fucked me again and again. He didn't cum, he just kept moving me from one position to the next, twisting and pulling my legs and spreading me impossibly wide. He was manic, claiming every orifice with his mouth, fingers, and cock. When he penetrated my ass he sunk his fingers deep into my pussy. I was full to bursting.

Today I feel like a stretched-out rubber band that's lost its elasticity. Swollen, gaping, worn out and hurting but... with the blissful memory of many, many orgasms. Antal didn't cum but I sure as shit did. Repeatedly.

When he finally exploded he sprayed me in my face right down to my thighs. Then he hugged me so tight we were glued together by his mess. Our night was intense, and neither of us got much sleep.

Walking into the Castle we're met with the sight of Csilla and Ladizsla practically dancing with excitement. They bombard me with questions asking *where have you been? why are you so late?* and enjoin me to *hurry, hurry up, he's waiting.*

Duna and the girls are curious and inclined to linger but Ladizsla sends them off to find Kartal to get their cleaning assignments.

Then Csilla tells us that a Royal courier arrived some time earlier to deliver a beautifully engraved invitation. It invites Princess Lake and her husband Anton Szémozsa along with Lord Sándor and his wife Csilla Koczinyi to attend an audience with Their Royal Highnesses at the Palace.

"He's waiting for your answer. We've been stalling him saying we couldn't think where you'd go to—"

"Or when you'd be back, but you're here now so come along–"

"Wait!" I cry, as Ladizsla grabs hold of my arm. I shake her off saying: "They can stuff their invitation where the sun don't shine. I'm not going."

The older woman gasps in shock but Csilla remains calm saying: "Now Tó, think of the wider implications..."

"No, there's nothing about them that makes me want–"

Her interruption silences me. "Tó, I'm thinking about Antal. This will only help him. Believe me, the police will think twice before arresting a guest of Their Majesties."

I turn to my husband for his direction and his answer is a surprise. "Do whatever feels right for you, Tó. This is your family and the history between you is vile. Whatever you choose is fine with me."

"But if this can help you–"

"I'm not really worried. I know I'm innocent and our powerful friends will protect us until I can prove it."

My anger is swept away in a rush of gratitude for this marvelous man. He's putting my feelings ahead of his safety. He's putting me first.

I'm speechless as emotion overwhelms me but I get myself under control. My voice has barely a quiver as I reply: "Well if you're sure then of course we'll go. If we don't I'll always be left wondering what might have been. Csilla, where have you stashed this man. It is a man, isn't it?"

I can sense her relief as she gives me a smile and a nod before leading us down to a rarely used reception room. Hearing our footsteps in the flagstone corridor the equerry is standing at attention. He's older than all of us, even Ladizsla who is hovering outside the door. The man's uniform and bearing is so impressive. He actually clicks his heels! and bows to me but extends the thick creamy envelope to Csilla.

She accepts it with a half-curtsy and announces: "The Princess Lake has decided we will all be in attendance, as requested."

Despite the bland expression on his face the man somehow manages to convey an *of course she has* before bowing once again and backing out of the room. I have to hold back a giggle when I hear our eavesdropping Ladizsla quickly scuttle out of his way.

Throughout the whole encounter only Csilla had uttered a word. I comment that that was a weird little pantomime and Csilla assures me things will get weirder still.

"For a start this invitation will not only set out the time and date but it will include the protocols for how to behave in the presence of the Royals, how to address them, what is appropriate attire–"

"What, no yoga pants?"

Csilla's look of reproof fails to hide the smile struggling to break free. "What I mean is that it will explain things like *white gloves are required to be worn at all times.*"

"Ooh like those long gloves women wear to the opera? the kind that go right over the elbows?"

"Well yes, those for sure, but also gloves for the men. If the Royals deign to shake anybody's hand they don't want to touch our plebeian skin."

"Okay now I'm getting pissed off again."

"Don't, it's not worth it. Now open the invitation, just bend the seal and it will break."

I do as she says and pull out a gilt-edged invitation printed on heavy stock. It's covered in a thin tissue and I've never seen or felt such expensive paper. The lettering is embossed and so full of curls and swirls it's difficult to read. I skim over the words refusing to ever say their names out loud.

"Tó try to understand that these people have no real power except the homage we're willing to pay to them. Are they rich? sure, and people respect wealth, but their bloodline? not so much. Especially with their reputation."

The last phrase is muttered under her breath but I hear it and now I'm curious. "C'mon, Csilla spill."

"Spill?"

"Tell me what's going on with my maybe-not-so-illustrious relations. That's the second time someone has alluded to dark dealings."

"Who else did?"

"Actually it was Antal, responding to Sándor, but you were there too. It was when Erzsébet wanted to go into town shopping and Antal wouldn't let me go. You wondered if he was worried I'd be recognized–"

"Oh I do remember. Sándor commented about how no one suspected illegitimacy and Antal said *if they get a hint of scandal they won't hesitate to harm her. Tó stays here where she's safe.* I'll never forget that, it was such a shock to think of Antal actually caring that much about someone. About you, Tó."

"But he's not a bad man–"

"Oh sweetheart he really is. They all are. They're crime lords with plenty of blood on their hands. We don't have to like it but we do need to admit the truth to ourselves.

In addition Antal is known to be excessively cruel and honey we heard the flogging he gave you and you crying out."

In protest I assure her: "Antal treats me good–"

Csilla reaches over and lightly taps my lips. "I'm not judging you or him. All of our men have certain... traits, due to their dominant natures as shifter Alphas. Now that Antal has claimed you as his fated mate, plus married you, we will all support you in every way. And we won't let him be driven from his pack again, certainly not because of Beáta Majoros!"

"I want to kill her," I savagely declare.

"I can understand that, but you can't, otherwise Antal will be blamed for that death too."

I feel my face screw up in disappointment because what Csilla is saying is the truth. Speaking of which: "So you've avoided answering me but my question remains. What's the gossip about the Royal Family that people whisper about?"

Csilla gives me an annoyed little frown before accepting that I'm not gonna drop this topic. "Well, there's no proof or even strong suspicion,

120

if there was well... even the Royals aren't above the law, especially as far as the humans are concerned.

Nevertheless there has always been talk about the disappearances and deaths of the people who stood between this King and his throne. Also, how whenever someone becomes an enemy of the Queen they...vanish. But it's all just gossip!"

"Except we know, because of the way they treated me, that their hands aren't clean. My husband may be a criminal and okay, deep down he's a monster, but he's never done anything as fiendish as these people did."

Now Csilla's frown of annoyance turns to worry and she's quick to reassure me: "Oh Tó, we won't let anything happen to you at the Palace."

An Impromptu Party

T6

As soon as the Royal courier leaves Csilla and Ladiszla hurry to the front of the Castle to see what the workers have managed to get done. We're all surprised to discover most of the clean-up has already happened. Kinga is sweeping away the debris and Ilka is ferrying the full garbage bags out to the yard.

The smell of freshly cut lumber emanates from the entrance and we see where the windows and the great doors have been reinforced until the craftsmen can come and repair and restore.

The stone exterior of the Koczinyi Castle has withstood centuries of enemy attacks and continues to do so. Sándor spent a fortune modernizing the living quarters which Csilla has made so comfortable it's easy to forget all the ancient history.

By early afternoon the Castle is once again secure. Some things will need to be replaced but Csilla has plenty of time and there's no rush. Stained rugs have been rolled up to go to the cleaners and the blood has been scrubbed out of the floor. Holes in the walls have been plastered over, ready for painting.

A lot has been accomplished and it's been thirsty work. Everyone is ready for a break and the drinking begins while the servers bring out dish after dish and load up the trestle tables set out on the lawn.

Someone produces Bluetooth speakers which pair with a phone to deliver lively dance music. The young men and women who staff the Koczinyi household remove their aprons and undo a couple of shirt buttons as they whirl across the graveled drive, enjoying each other's company.

Even I'm tapping my foot to the beat and I'm not a dancer.

Turning to Antal to say *isn't this great?* I notice how tired my husband looks. There's a shady area away from the crowd so I lead him there and draw him to lie down on the grass with me. I place his head in my lap and smoothing his hair back from his forehead tell him to *aludj most, szerelmem [sleep now, my love]*. He doesn't fight me which shows how exhausted he is.

Sitting with my back against the wide trunk of an ancient oak tree I'm comfortable enough to doze. We've both been asleep for some time because when we waken it's evening. Antal lifts his upper body just enough to slide me down beneath him. In the dim light I see him staring at me with a serious expression before he pecks a kiss to my lips and jumps to his feet pulling me up with him.

"I'm starving!" he declares.

I don't need to answer because we both know I'm always hungry. We head towards the refreshments attracted by the delicious spicy smell of roasted meats. The food has been replenished and there's a vast selection.

I'm still cautious with local dishes I can't identify, the paprika can be so hot! but I recognize *chicken paprikash* and know it's made with the sweet variety of the spice.

After filling our plates we drift apart as Antal spots his brother chatting with Grigor, and I see Gyuri's wife, Réka, sitting with her feet propped up.

"Hey Mama-to-be," I greet her.

She grins back at me saying: "I've just been hearing about the fancy invitation you received."

Her sister Marta joins us, carrying two plates. She hands one to Réka before asking: "What fancy invitation is this?"

"Ugh! a Royal Audience," I grunt with a scowl.

"At the Palace of the Jagiellons? Wow!" Marta's impressed and I realize she knows nothing of my history. Réka sends a slight nod my way encouraging me to elaborate.

I take a deep breath and in a rush explain: "I'm actually Princess Lake, Prince River is my twin, and the King and Queen are my parents. So-called."

Marta's mouth is hanging open as are another couple of women I don't know but who have come close to listen. *Did you hear that? The King and Queen! She's a Princess* I hear someone murmur.

Before everyone starts asking questions I hurry to say: "I've never met them, they abandoned me as an infant, left me to die but... I didn't. This meeting might be all about them wanting to finish me off." Which effectively ends the conversation.

Moving away from the wives I gravitate to the staff. The casual group I join up with is more to my liking. They're sitting around a dying fire debating whether or not they should fire it up again. Potatoes were tossed into the embers and I'm invited to help myself. Crouching down I grab one, take a bite and it's delicious!

Looking up I see Antal watching me so I ask if I can take another potato for him and I'm told *take as many as you like!* Thanking them I hurry over to my husband with my offering but he shakes his head.

"Don't you want one? They're so good!"

"No, I like my potatoes in vodka."

"Is that still a thing? making vodka from potatoes?"

"Oh yeah, you can still get it. You eat and I'll drink, how's that?"

"And we'll both be merry!" I laugh and he throws his arm across my shoulders pulling me into his side. He and Gyuri pick up their conversation and I'm happy just to be there with them. Soon we are joined by Sándor, Kartal, and Grigor.

Gyuri neatly cuts me away from the other men but we only move a few steps. "Welcome to our family, *sógornőm [sister-in-law]* Tó."

"Thank you, *sógor [brother-in-law]* Gyuri," I reply.

Gyuri has a booming laugh and I can't help but join in when he lets loose. "Wonderful! you have been studying our language?"

"Yes, but I also heard someone refer to Kada as my brother-in-law which is how I learned the word."

"Ah, yes. Kada would have– you never met him, did you?"

"No, but I saw him at the party at the Castle. Not to speak to or anything but... well I couldn't help but notice him pulling his wife out of the room. I didn't know who they were and after that scene I didn't want to."

Shaking his head with a resigned look on his face Gyuri explains that his elder brother did not have a happy marriage. "I've been blessed myself, and I hope the same happiness for you and my baby brother."

The thought of Antal being a *baby brother* makes me giggle and Gyuri smiles at me before continuing: "It's so good to see how happy Antal is with you. You're exactly right for him and, based on the way the two of you can't take your eyes off each other, I'd say he's definitely the right one for you, too."

I surprise myself by responding quickly and from the heart: "Antal is my everything."

"I've really missed my brother for all these years. I look forward to the day we celebrate Antal's return to the Szémozsa pack and your initiation."

I guess my expression is apprehensive because he hurries to reassure me that it's a lot of fun. "It's exciting to join a pack as a member's mate. You'll participate in one of our runs and when Antal catches you he'll mark you with a bite. Which he's already done once, and will do so again and again. It's a ritual we all enjoy."

"I've only recently started going on runs but I love them! I don't know if you know, but I wasn't raised as a wolf... I discovered my dual nature the hard way - at puberty when it could no longer be denied!

I still have so much to learn, but your initiation does sound like a fun ritual. However Antal is adamant he will not ask you to lift the banishment until his name is cleared."

"You're a good wife, Tó, to say *adamant* instead of calling it *pigheaded stubbornness*."

I smell Antal's scent just as his arms snake around my stomach and he pulls me close. "My brother has been monopolizing you and now it's my turn to reclaim what is mine before he insults me again."

Tilting my head back I meet his gaze and we share a smile. I love how much more relaxed he is and how easily that beautiful smile lights up his face. It must be because he's back in his homeland.

Out of the darkness a rich baritone sings a melancholy tune. It's heartbreaking. Although I can understand most of the words it's not the lyrics that stir my soul but the way the sound evokes such a longing inside me. I've never had such a visceral reaction to music in my whole life.

Antal hears the small sob that escapes me and cupping my cheek tilts my face up to meet his gaze. I see the sheen of unshed tears in his eyes and know that he too is deeply affected. Looking around in the sudden stillness I feel an empathy with all the shifters here. Ahhh, that's it. The music calls to our wolves, making them yearn to break free from our human forms.

There's a long silence after the song ends and we all breath a collective sigh.

"Who was that?" I ask in wonder. Gyuri mundanely answers *the chef* as if everyone knows that. I'm completely taken aback I mean *seriously, the chef?*

He chuckles at the look on my face explaining: "Ferenc is famous around here as *The Singing Chef.* People have told him he should go on that European talent show and you know what he says?"

Now Gyuri gives another deep belly laugh before continuing: "He says *if I enter a singing contest I'll win and then they'll expect me to always be singing so when will I have time to cook?*"

Csilla joins us then adding: "And he's simply the best cook, the best chef we've ever had, so we don't want to lose him."

The haunting melody fades and then a group starts up in a folk song that involves clapping, timed pauses, and feet stomping. Soon the night air echoes with the happy sounds of fun and celebration.

Drinking, cheers, kisses... we've had a full day and tonight has been magical.

Erzsébet's Apology

Tó

"Erzsébet insists on seeing you so we're going to drive you to Janos' home. He won't let her travel since she's suffering from car sickness right now. It's really just morning sickness but it is awful to be away from your own home when you feel poorly."

"I've never been to their place, but I know where it is, it's just a short trip," comments Antal.

"That's right and we'll take the scenic route along the river to let Tó see a bit more of our town."

After a pleasant journey the four of us arrive at the Erdős compound. The Erdős pack is relatively small, but wealthy and its success is reflected in their homes. I'm not surprised to see that the style of Janos and Erzsébet's home is distinctive, ultramodern architecture.

The front door opens and Janos is waving us in before Máté has even parked the car. After handshakes and kisses he leads our group into a big open room with large windows covered in yellow sheers which gives the space a golden glow.

Erzsébet's remains seated on the couch. Her stomach is only slightly rounded, but pregnancy is evident in the fullness of her breasts and the softness of her face. Her whole demeanor has changed from prickly sarcasm to sweet calm, except that now she looks sorrowful.

"First of all you need to understand that I had no idea – never imagined for one moment – that my silly social media post would go viral. Actually first I should say I'm sorry because I really am." Erzsébet's words come straight from her heart, her sincerity obvious.

"Tó and Antal, I apologize for all the trouble I caused. I did it to spite the Royal Family, not you two." She gestures towards us, hesitant to reach out, but when I take hold of the older woman's hand she clutches my fingers in relief.

"Antal knew the posts identifying him could never have come from you–"

Erzsébet is quick to agree. "That's true! I never mentioned, I never would, his name or business or anything like that. Believe me Janos was so mad at me because of what came out after others started digging. He told me I had to fix things or else! I finally had to admit I was pregnant so he wouldn't beat me–"

"Janos!" I exclaim in horror, "I never want you to beat Erzsébet on my behalf, are we clear?"

The man raises an eyebrow at the idea of a little Omega like me telling him what to do. We both catch the scowl on Antal's face and know my insolence will be dealt with later by my husband. I sigh, and Antal smirks.

Lifting his other eyebrow to give me a look of sham innocence Janos explains:

"After all our time together Erzsébet is well-acquainted with my disciplinary measures. I do not *beat* her, I administer the corporal punishment decreed by our pack lore. But our laws allow for leniency when the miscreant is expecting. We never put a whelp at risk. Of course pregnancy wouldn't – and didn't – save her from a sound spanking by my hand."

Turning to Antal he adds: "Rest assured Erzsébet will not make that mistake again."

Still wearing his trademark Alpha-hole smirk Antal nods before replying: "Actually, we might need her to do it again."

I silently applaud Antal's dry delivery when I see the startled look on their faces. It's fun to see how he's caught them by surprise. "Maybe Erzsébet could explain her part in all this and then we can figure out how best to use that?" I suggest.

Csilla calmly states: "It's always a good idea to start at the beginning."

Motioning us all to sit down Erzsébet starts off by repeating her apology. Then she says: "I have an Auntie who works for the Royal Family. She's completely steeped in their lifestyle and thinks the sun shines out of their collective butts. They treat her terribly, but that's no different from the way they treat everyone else.

The pay is disgraceful, the hours are deplorable, but the prestige and chance to bask in the aura of the regal bloodline is supposed to somehow make up for that." Erzsébet shakes her head, truly puzzled over her aunt's starstruck behavior.

"She has some grand title but absolutely nothing else. They could dismiss her tomorrow and she would be left destitute with no where to go. Despite all that Auntie is completely infatuated and constantly brags to my mother and me about all their doings."

Erzsébet shifts in her seat and her husband lifts her legs, placing her feet in his lap. He pulls off the slippers she's wearing and begins a massage starting with her toes. Erzsébet sigh is both relief and pleasure. Addressing me she continues her story.

"Somehow the Royals were notified when you made an inquiry about your birth certificate. Auntie probed her confidantes for information because she hadn't even known of your existence and she's a very nosy woman. I'm afraid the stories made you out to be something evil and vile.

When Prince River failed in his mission to eliminate you the rumors turned even blacker. Especially when he came home bearing deep scars on his arm. They made him take a rabies shot, actually a series of them."

"Oh I've heard that's a terribly painful treatment," Csilla puts in.

I nod and say *good!*

Erzsébet chuckles at the expression on my face. "From that point on you were always watched, but at a distance. I think they were looking for an opportunity to kill you but of course that was never said out loud. Our Royal Family deserves the bloody reputation it's earned itself, Tó, and they are feared."

Antal isn't much for PDAs but he does give me a wink.

Csilla catches it and laughs lightly. "That's why Antal wouldn't let you go shopping with us that day, remember? Too many people at the party commented on your unusual eye color. Over here it's practically synonymous with the Jagiellons and he rightly believed talk about a connection might put you in danger."

Of course I recall exactly what Csilla is talking about. Antal forbade me to leave and I obeyed him without question.

I don't need to thwart him in order to get a punishment, hurting me is something he enjoys, so I usually do what he says. Usually... sometimes I feel his demons rising within and know that it's better to bleed off a little mania to prevent a full-blown explosion. And it's far more enjoyable to play the role of submissive by choice rather than coercion.

I enjoy the role-play. It takes me out of myself and lets my mind escape from the pain being inflicted at the hands of the man I've come to love. There I've admitted it to myself. I do love Antal and I think he has grown to love me as well. We're such a macabre, grisly couple... I think we deserve each other. I mentally give myself to shake to get back into the conversation.

"So when my brother came to our home in America he didn't realize we'd been in Hungary? the family had just heard stories and then your social media post was brought to their attention?"

"That's what we think happened but we can't know for sure. I only meant to poke a hole through their *façade* but wow, they are even more hated than I realized! My post got shared over and over again until some eNews outlets and influencers scooped it up and created a *cause célèbre*."

"And then somebody dug deeper and uncovered Antal's involvement so suddenly my wife's notoriety put us in trouble with our syndicate."

"Mmm, yes. I was forced to confess my part to Janos and then tell him about the pregnancy. I'd held off because well... in the past we, we–" Her husband shushes her stutter with a kiss.

"We all kept a close eye on the items which grew wilder and more speculative with each new theory. But you know," here Sándor pauses and looks everyone in the eye before saying: "Nothing was as bad as the truth. I mean, the fact that you were literally dumped in the street to die is horrific. I'm afraid I've lost all respect for that family and yet they've been figureheads my entire life."

I'm sure my eyes cloud over as I fall into a trance of memory. Recovering a few moments later I say: "Someone wasn't fully on board with their plan."

At the curious looks I continue: "I was found with a note saying *Her name is Lake* and if I hadn't had that information to go on I would have applied for my paperwork as a *Jane Doe*. None of this would have come about."

They all consider the implications of a betrayal by someone very close and very trusted. This person must have been part of the plot that saw them travel thousands of miles to abandon an unwanted baby to certain death and burial as an *unidentified infant* far away from her birthplace.

"Erzsébet, do you think you could leak news of our invitation to the Palace tomorrow night? Maybe make a big deal about crediting the several social media outlets for making this happen. That should get them full of self-congratulation and enough goodwill to share it on."

"Oh, that's a great idea, Tó. The post will practically write itself... I'll write it out now and you can have a read before I publish it. And if you like I can post separately about the ridiculous accusation against Antal, see if we can't rally some support for him."

Both Antal and I reflect on this new idea for a bit but decide to hold off right now. "I'm hoping the authorities come to their senses and drop the charge so I think we should probably avoid rousing any additional interest. But if the police are stupid and stubborn then sure, that will be great." He and I share a satisfied smile, our plan to clear his name is moving forward.

Antal's phone dings with an incoming text and after reading it he asks: "Does anyone know a club called *Szexi Róka [Sexy Fox]* or where it is? I just a got message from Imre saying he's got news and wants to meet me–" He breaks off at Sándor's snort of disgust. "What?"

Csilla lays a restraining hand on her husband's forearm before answering: "It's a gay bar and if you're going Tó must stay behind, she

133

won't be welcome. It's in a bad area so have Máté drive you and take Grigor as well."

I wonder why she doesn't suggest that Kartal join the party?

"It's not a bad area," Janos reasons, "but a gay club isn't popular with the locals and patrons of the venue have been beaten up."

"Can you blame–" begins Sándor but Csilla sharply interjects: "Stop! Homosexuality is legal husband-of-mine and you need to open your mind and rein in your prejudices."

Everyone is taken aback at Csilla's sharp retort. She's normally so demure and agreeable that it's easy to forget she's an Alpha. Sándor's lips are drawn into a thin line as if he's forcibly holding back his words.

He scowls as Csilla goes on to explain: "Sándor's nephew recently *came out of the closet* and I'm afraid the men of the family find this news upsetting."

"How old-fashioned of them! I'm guessing the women are okay with it?" asks Erzsébet.

"The women all knew long before Bence ever admitted it out loud. So yes, we're okay with it because he's family and we love him." Turning to Sándor with a frown she adds: "You've always said Bence is a wonderful young man and a credit to the Koczinyi name."

Spluttering her husband expostulates: "That was before I knew–"

"No!" interrupts Csilla again, snapping out her words: "Nothing has changed. Bence's sex life is none of our business but his place in our family as our nephew demands our support for whatever choices he makes. Your thoughts on this matter are out-of-date, Sándor." Her eyes are flashing and her husband wisely withholds further comment.

"Soooo," I ask in a bratty tone, "should Antal wear anything special to this place?"

Kartal cracks us all up saying: "No, just his usual leather and gold chains."

Antal growls, but he's smiling. "Imre tells me Stefan will be there as well. I should see if Gyuri wants to join us, we all used to hang out together."

"Antal, Gyuri won't go to a place like that. He'd be concerned about rumors being spread about his marriage."

"Are you serious?" I'm stunned by this narrowmindedness.

"Tó you don't understand pack life–"

"I refuse to believe all shifters are hetero."

"No, of course not, but they usually join a pack of, of... like-minded wolves. With male Omegas. Females, I mean lesbians, are expected to be bi-sexual at least during their reproductive years. You won't know this Tó but our population has an extremely low birth rate." Janos pulls Erzsébet closer proudly resting his hand on her belly.

"Yes, why is that? What's changed? I'm one of four, three of us male, which was a bit unusual among the families we grew up with but not really strange or anything," comments Antal.

I'm surprised to hear that Antal has a sister and ask about her.

"Ilona. She was a little girl when I left, but as a prized Omega she's since married into Croatian shifter nobility and lives on the Dalmatian Coast."

"So you haven't seen her in years..." I begin and Csilla suggests we have Gyuri arrange a video call. The idea brings one of Antal's rare smiles to his face.

"Getting back to our fertility issues... our doctors suspect a virus that sterilizes she-wolves."

"And we believe it's man-made, too."

I look from face to face seeing worry, concern, even anger. Could a planned genocide of our kind possibly be true? "But that's... Who would do—"

"We think it came from the States. The U.S. has become one of the least shifter-friendly countries."

"This prejudice is a far cry from America's beginnings, you know: *give me your tired, your poor, your huddled masses yearning to breathe free.*"

"Which is why it's more important than ever that all our young men and women mate and marry," declares Sándor decisively.

Csilla merely gives her head a shake before standing to say to Antal: "Máté can take us home, pick up Grigor, then take you to meet Imre. I expect you'll be having a late night so we'll hear the news in the morning and I'll call you, Erzsébet."

Her Highness Princess Lake

Csilla

I don't have time for this old fool, I think eyeing Senior Detective-Inspector László Garai with barely concealed impatience. *Can't he see we've got our hands full with the on-going repairs and clean up? Yet there he sits, full of self-importance, fussing over his stupid notepad. He licks his finger to turn the page... ugh!*

I'm not in the best of moods and haven't offered him any refreshment in the hope he'll take the hint, but no such luck. He doesn't leave so in my firmest voice I say: "You really must come back when my husband is here, sir. I know he will want to speak with you."

"Ah yes, that's excellent, excellent. I look forward to meeting Sándor Koczinyi very much." Leaning back in his chair he casts an appreciative eye around the room, cataloging and admiring our possessions. His covetous study gives the impression he'd like to get up and handle everything, leaving his fingerprints all over.

"But Madame, I have questions for you as well and maybe by time we're through your good husband will have returned. Perhaps?"

I don't understand why he's doing this, especially since we recently heard from Marta Pataky that he's not supposed to be actively involved in this investigation. I'm struggling to hang on to my temper.

I hear voices in the hall and think *oh no! that must be Tó what am I going to do—?* when Garai stands and before I'm out of my chair he's already moving towards the doorway. He's quicker than you'd think from his age and appearance.

Ladiszla appears in the room first, ushering in Tó, and then bending into a curtsy and murmuring *Your Highness.*

Tó, looking as non-plussed as I feel, barely glances at the old servant before looking at Garai then turning towards me. I'm inspired to imitate Ladiszla's over-the-top behavior and also curtsy, praying Tó doesn't snort out a belly-laugh at me. She doesn't, she takes the hint and regally inclines her head when I respectfully say *Princess.*

We both look at Garai and I introduce him to her as: "László Garai, from the Police."

"Senior Detective-Inspector Garai, at your service ma'am." He jerks out a bow in a ludicrous performance. My lips twitch but Tó is magnificent.

With a slow blink – as if she's studying some alien species – she pauses for a long moment before stating: "I am Princess Lake."

When Garai offers his hand to shake she lifts an eyebrow and quietly, as though speaking to herself, says: "I realize Hungary is a Republic but surely..." and trails off, ignoring him after that.

"Csilla, I apologize for interrupting, I didn't realize you have company. We'll meet up later."

She turns to leave but Garai makes a big production of showing her to a chair and exclaiming *she mustn't be inconvenienced by him* as he seats her.

"I've heard rumors of a long-lost Princess of the House Jagiellon... a different bloodline from my ancestors of course, but an honor, most definitely an honor to make your acquaintance, ma'am."

He's obviously delighted to be in the company of nobility – for the Koczinyi family are aristocrats – and royalty – even if the Jagiellons *are* shifters.

I expect Tó to make some remark but she simply wears an expressionless face and looks from one of us to the other.

"Inspector Garai was saying he's here to ask me some questions, but I don't know what this is about." Now we both turn his way and see him visibly straighten his spine, full of authority.

"By your leave," he pompously declaims to Tó before giving his attention back to me. "I have questions about the evening of November 20 when you had people here for a soiree, I believe?"

When I nod he continues: "I'm sure you have since heard that one of the guests, Kada Szémozsa, was brutally murdered that very same night?"

Again I merely nod so he explains: "I'd like to know what time this guest arrived, when he left, and anything you can tell me about his visit, interactions, what you observed, and your own conversation with him."

With his pen poised he leans forward to write down my answers. This silly nuisance of a man. I pause so he thinks I'm giving his questions full consideration.

"I didn't see the Szémozsas arrive, I only noticed them for a moment before they left just before 9:00, and I didn't speak to either of them."

He scoffs at my answer questioning: "How can you be so certain what time they left? Especially if you didn't even speak to these guests?"

I dryly reply: "Everyone knows when they left because, as usual, Kada and Beáta Szémozsa put on a little family drama and got everybody's attention. I don't what occurred to set him off, but suddenly he's grabbed hold of her wrist and is dragging her out the door as she protests and he yells.

I no longer invite the Szémozsas into my home for this very reason. They create scenes and don't socialize well, but they came along with another couple who were invited. As I say I have no idea what time they arrived but I'm positive about when they left. No doubt someone videoed the debacle on their phone which will also give confirmation."

It's obvious he's surprised by my information. Surprised and annoyed from the look on his face. With narrowed eyes he turns to Tó saying: "You were here as well, weren't you Princess? I mean, you are also Mrs. Antal Szémozsa, aren't you?"

"Yes, I am," Tó replies in a voice without inflection and an equally bland look on her face.

"Where is your husband? is he in Hungary now? Is he here at the Castle? I want to interview him. But first, did you also witness this alleged scene between Mr. and Mrs... oh! your in-laws, I presume?"

"Yes, I saw the woman manhandled out the door by an angry man who I later learned was her husband, but I didn't know either of them. We weren't introduced, and I wasn't yet married."

"Did you know that here in Hungary we don't have that law about a wife not being able to testify against her husband–" he begins, but Tó interrupts him.

"We don't in the States, either."

The man sputters an argument but she continues: "A wife *can* testify if she chooses, she just can't be *compelled* by the court to do so."

Garai scowls silently for a bit before continuing: "You didn't answer me about your husband–"

Fortunately before he can go any further with his questions we all hear my husband's booming voice in the hall demanding: "What's this I hear about a Royal Courier and us being invited to the Palace tomorrow?" as he strides into the room.

The two of us have been on the outs ever since our argument regarding his nephew Bence and I'm still angry, but profoundly relieved to have him take over this interview with László Garai.

Tó

Thank fuck Sándor's arrived before I lose it with this cop. This is the asshole behind all the harassment of Antal, I silently fume. He hounded a teenager out of the country years ago and he's still doing his best to ruin Antal's life. My wolf is clamoring to be set free to savage this man. I wholeheartedly wish I could just let her loose!

I've been holding myself upright and motionless, a stance I learned to adopt when Antal suffers a mood swing. I efface myself to hide from his attention even though that mostly doesn't work. Still, I play statues to avoid provoking him. Now this loser is testing my self-control and I'm on the verge of saying something I shouldn't. I force myself to take a deep breath, be unemotional, and get back to listening to the conversation.

He and Sándor are arguing or rather Sándor is berating the man who is trying to justify himself.

Csilla stands and I do too so we can leave. As I turn to go the pig calls to me: "Princess! Where were you and your husband – pardon, your *fiancé* – up until midnight on the 20th?"

I slowly turn back to face him. Mustering up all the icy calm I can, I coolly answer: "We were here at the Castle until the Koczinyis kindly drove us to the airfield. They stayed until we boarded our jet for a scheduled ten o'clock flight back to the States. We left on time, which means we were high in the sky at midnight."

When he tries to ask if I'm sure about that I ignore him and walk out of the room with Csilla close behind. I can still hear him, his voice sounding desperate, calling *where is Antal Szémozsa now?*

As soon as we're in the hallway Csilla whispers: "Tó! You were wonderful, so regal. You sure put that little worm in his place."

I almost collapse against her as we link arms for support. "Csilla I was so scared. That's the man who is trying to put Antal in prison. I wanted to sic my wolf on him. I still want to do that! Does he not understand not to push shifters too far? I mean, it's taking everything I have to hold back."

She squeezes my arm in agreement then adds in a fervent voice: "At least Antal is safely out with the boys and will be gone for hours."

Imre Gets the Goods

Antal

The *Szexi Róka [Sexy Fox]* is located on the outskirts of a commercial district that borders a residential neighborhood.

A heavily-muscled bouncer guards the door, and the few smokers indulging their habit stick close by him. The three of us are carefully watched as we approach and the man's expression isn't welcoming.

I greet him by stating: "Imre Pék invited us." He steps to the side and pulls open the door but doesn't say anything. Beside him someone mutters *szerencsés [lucky] Imre.*

The club décor is fashionable with its muted colors and Art Deco styling. A DJ plays techno dance music at such a high volume the room reverberates with the bass.

Imre has been watching for me and waves us over to the bar. His lips are moving, but I can't hear him over the noise. Stefan is there, wearing his usual sneering expression, but he shakes hands all round. We order our drinks and follow Imre past the dance-floor to a quieter area with comfortable seating.

Imre is wearing eye make-up and it gives him an edgy *bad boy* look, especially with his carefully barbered scruff. Stefan sits like he's posing for a camera and I remember that he used to do some modeling and maybe still does? He's certainly got the looks. He's never been much of a talker but he's leaning in to listen to Imre's conversation with me.

"I dropped in at the house, as we discussed, to offer my condolences along with a bottle of Pálinka–"

"Beáta was never much of a drinker," I interpose.

"That was true back then, but now? now she's known to be a thirsty woman. I knew she'd welcome a drink and would invite me to join her. So anyhow, after we got past all the pious, maudlin bullshit she let the brandy do the talking.

Antal we knew your brother was a Class A prick when we were kids and he sure didn't improve with age. Once she got started on his list of faults Beáta held nothing back. She hated her husband and no wonder.

Kada had girlfriends he took out publicly, financed a luxurious lifestyle for a young mistress, constantly criticized and humiliated Beáta, and then beat her if she complained. Of course we only have her word for it now—"

"No, even I heard stories about him beating on her," interrupts Stefan, pausing to muse: "Although I don't know why anyone would think I cared."

Imre just shakes his head with a smile at his friend before continuing.

"She called the sex *marital rape* and started to say something about *she should have known* but stopped and I couldn't get her to say anything further about that.

The only good thing she said about Kada is that he was generous with her allowance and the money he gave her parents each month. Of course that money was the proceeds from the pack's enterprises, but he liked to play the big shot with it."

"I have no trouble believing that," I comment, and I'm sure my tone is bitter. Grigor's narrowed eyes show he shares my contempt.

"The important stuff came out at the end of the conversation. Well, she was so drunk by then she couldn't stop herself from talking. She admitted she *might have been muddled about what time the killing occurred* and *maybe her mind got confused about seeing you at her house*, and *possibly she got mixed up after having seen you for the first time in years earlier that night.*"

"Oh Imre, that's excellent! thank you."

Máté heard about Beáta's accusation against me from Csilla and now he states: "So it's the widow's word against yours, Antal; my Alphas; and now Imre. I don't see how the police can even consider proceeding, they don't have a case."

"Oh it's not just my word," says Imre with a pleased, excited giggle. "I recorded her on my phone!"

"Is that legal here?" I ask incredulously.

"It doesn't matter if it can't be used in court, the knowledge that it exists – and is *leakable* to the Press – will be enough to make the prosecutor back off," he finishes triumphantly.

I recall that he never liked Beáta and neither did Stefan who says: "You got the bitch good!" and the two high five each other.

"We need another round of drinks and they're on me!" I happily announce waving a server over. His costume makes me blink but other than that I keep my face impassive. I don't know if Imre chose this venue to unnerve me or to keep Tó out of the way. It doesn't matter, I'm so fucking pleased with what he achieved I'll overlook any of his little mind games.

"Hey! Send that audio file to my phone now before we get too drunk to remember." A moment later the notification dings and I pass my phone to Grigor saying: "Take a copy for yourself, too."

We continue drinking and our conversation turns silly. At some point I'm heading to the bar but get waylaid onto the dance floor.

145

Me. Dancing. In. A. Gay. Bar.

But I'm with the boys from my youth and we're laughing, singing, drinking, dancing... and the exhilaration of proving Beáta lied to the police has made me lightheaded in celebration. I'm enjoying having fun with my familiar, old friends from way back.

A heavily intoxicated Imre, practically hanging off me with his arm flung around my neck, begs my forgiveness and promises he will always treat my wife respectfully.

I remember Grigor taking pictures on his phone and me asking *are you gonna blackmail me?* but before he can answer I blow him a kiss.

"Tó is going to love these!" he laughs.

The Morning After

Tó

"You had a rowdy time last night at that club, hmm? I recognize a hangover when I see one and I have no sympathy for you at all. You stood me up last night. I was looking forward to you and me celebrating, but by time you rolled in you were legless. Couldn't even focus. You're lucky Máté put you to bed because I'd have left you on the floor. God knows where Grigor slept."

Antal scowls at me as I run my mouth at him. One look at his handsome face colorless and drawn with lines of headache pain confirms that I'm safe from retribution. Serves him right.

He growls a complaint about wives who nag instead of giving comfort. Heaving a theatrical sigh I go off in search of Kartal for medication. He's way ahead of me. Seems the whole household heard the men come home so Kartal rightly guessed the situation and has brewed up some concoction which he promises will cure a hangover.

Sniffing the drink I pull back with disgust asking: "Does it taste as bad as it smells?"

"Worse!" he smugly replies and we smile at each other in righteous sobriety. I think I know why he didn't go to the club with the other three. Sándor's homophobia must be a challenge because Kartal was always *very* open-minded when he joined us during my heats.

Antal moans when presented with the drink which I tell him he has to down quickly before getting the pain-killers. He grumbles but complies giving me an evil look when his throat almost sends the liquid straight back up. That look means trouble is coming my way so I deflect by changing tactics.

I give him the two pills and a drink of water before gently pushing him back down on the bed, and settling his head in my lap. I lean against the headboard and lightly run my fingers across his forehead from his eyebrows to the crown of his head, soothing his pain. I gently scratch his scalp and stroke through his hair. I don't know any lullabyes but I hum a made-up tune until he falls back asleep.

It's late afternoon when everyone gathers to hear what Imre had to say. Grigor plays the audio of Beáta's recorded confession that Imre captured on his phone. We hear how she slurs her words from the heavy drinking but I can't feel sorry for her when she spits out such nasty spite and venom.

"Well that's conclusive," states Sándor with satisfaction. "I know it wasn't legally obtained but we don't need to take it into a courtroom because once the *Államügyész [District Attorney]* hears it he'll know there's no case."

Janos reaches for the phone so he can replay the clip. I notice that Janos wears the same expression of grim pleasure that I see on Sándor's face. Erzsébet takes the phone from him and after watching the video nosily scrolls through the rest of the images.

I'm surprised to see my husband rub his forehead. Surely he isn't still feeling hangover effects?

I give him a quizzical look and he answers saying: "I'm just... just wondering what the hell happened to Beáta? Was it her marriage that turned her into this cruel, poisonous woman or was that always part of her nature?"

"Antal, I think Beáta and Kada brought out the worst in each other," comments Csilla. "Theirs wasn't an arranged marriage but neither did they marry for love. Beáta was a beauty but I think the real attraction she held for Kada was the fact that she was yours. And as for her?

I guess she thought the status of being the Pack Leader's wife would satisfy her but obviously it didn't. Neither one fulfilled the other."

"Don't sympathize with her, *szerelmem [my love]*," says Sándor. "She's done a terrible thing and then compounded her crime by incriminating an innocent man."

That sobering thought makes us all pause until Erzsébet startles everyone by loudly snorting. Her eyes are bright and her mouth wide open as she holds up Grigor's phone and laughs.

"What the hell did you guys get up to last night?" she splutters, looking down at some photos on the phone and howling with glee.

Her husband takes the phone from her and she warns: "Don't let Sándor see it! Sándor don't look, we know how you feel about gays–"

Of course I bounce right over beside them so I can look. Just as Sándor begins saying *what are you talking about?* I squeal "OMIGOD Antal, Imre's giving you tongue in this shot, and oh look he and Stefan have you sandwiched between them and they're both grinding on you."

With a frown of annoyance Antal snaps: "That doesn't sound right–" but Máté pipes up: "Oh yes, everyone was cheering you on when you were dancing. Don't you remember?"

I clap my hands exclaiming: "I sure wish I'd been there and seen that! Antal flaunting it on the dance-floor under the colored lights... oooh! was there a disco ball? Were there black lights turning clothes fluorescent?"

Erzsébet stirs things up even more by commenting: "I can't imagine anyone would forget that package being pushed into them..."

I look at a video of Stefan holding Antal from behind, his arms wrapped around my husband's neck, while Imre is thrusting his dick, visibly hard through his pants, up and down against Antal's groin. I feel my eyebrows stretching up to my hairline and I can't contain the giggles that bubble up.

Grigor looks sheepishly at his Alpha who complains: "You're supposed to protect me from this sort of thing. Fuck knows who else had their phones out..."

"Sorry! but I was doing shots with the rest of you."

Turning to Máté Grigor says accusingly: "This is your fault. You were the driver so you were sober." But Máté flips him off.

Antal scowls at me so I won't think he's ashamed of himself but I find the whole thing hilarious. If my laughter is slightly hysterical I figure it's relief that Antal's ordeal with the police will soon be over.

I decide I'll wait till he's feeling better before telling him about the visit from Inspector Garai.

A Royal Audience

Tó

I give myself over entirely to Csilla's maid who is either a witch or a magician because once again she makes me up and styles my hair to perfection.

My gown has a modest cut but it's exactly what I imagine a real princess would wear. I mean supposedly I already am a real princess but I sure don't feel like one... although in this dress? maybe.

It's all-white with lacy short sleeves and a lace-covered bodice that sits high on my chest showing not even a hint of cleavage. It's fitted down to my waist and then it flares to three times my width with layers and layers of tulle and chiffon and something else that Csilla mentioned but I've forgotten the name. It sways and swishes when I move. With white gloves covering my arms past my elbows I'm showing very little skin.

I can't stop looking at myself in the mirror! I could pass for the Bride figurine on top of a wedding cake.

It wasn't all that long ago I was scrawny from undernourishment, with a pink nose from a chronic sniffle, and performing drudge work in the kitchen where I made myself a corner to sleep. Now I really look like the princess everyone claims me to be.

Antal walks into the room fully recovered from his over-indulgence and wearing a smirk on his face. When I see how he's dressed I understand why. He's decked out entirely in white, white on white, except for his polished black shoes and a maroon sash banded with gold trim.

He quirks an eyebrow at me and I start to giggle. After all my teasing that I'd be *salivating rapturously over his good looks offset by a black tuxedo* I'm forced to admit that he's utterly devastating in white.

"I didn't know there was such a thing as white tuxes!" I exclaim. "Is this a European fashion? Let me feel it."

The material is a lightweight brocade with satin lapels that match his bowtie and a shirt of skinny pleats. The sash has a medallion but I don't know what the insignia means. Something to identify his family, I guess. I think I should get to wear something like that now that I'm legally a member of his family, too. Unless it's just for the men?

I might not truly believe I'm a princess but right now I feel like a real-life Cinderella. The dress makes me graceful and beautiful and... like I'm somebody. When I'm on my husband's arm and held close by his side I know exactly who I am: Mrs. Antal Szémozsa.

Announcing: "This was just delivered by a Royal courier." Csilla comes in then stops with a gasp. "Tó! Antal! just look at you two... you're the best-looking couple I've ever seen!"

She's holding a tissue-wrapped package that she now opens to reveal an aquamarine sash. Csilla drapes it over my shoulder and smooths the satin to hang across my chest down to my hip.

"Do I have to wear this?" I ask. "I'd rather have Antal's colors."

"Tó," Csilla bites her lip and casts an apologetic look at my husband before saying: "You outrank Antal so yes, you do have to wear the Jagiellon Royal Sash. This is the proper color for your family."

He pinches my cheek and turns me to look at our reflections in the full-length mirror. It's true, we do make a stunning couple. His sandy-brown hair, dark eyes and swarthy complexion contrasts so dramatically with my platinum locks and pale skin. The blue of the sash accentuates my eyes which sparkle with delight. A delicate pink blush rises up from my chest to stain my cheeks when I encounter Antal's heated gaze.

"*Olyan jóképű vagy [You are so handsome]*," I tell him.

Csilla has come round to stand between us and the mirror while she snaps photos on her phone. When Antal takes hold of my chin to tip my face up for a kiss I know that no matter what happens tonight nothing will top this magical moment. My cheeks hurt I'm grinning so widely and my heart aches with the fullness of... something. I'll think about what that *something* means later.

Leading us out of our suite Csilla calls to Sándor that we're ready. The older Alpha presents a distinguished look in his traditional black tuxedo brightened by a gold braided sash wrapped several times around his waist. He lays a square of the same material over Csilla's shoulder and pins it in place with a brooch of their family crest.

Ladiszla has followed him in and now fusses over each of their outfits, straightening a tie here and brushing off imaginary fluffs there. The older woman is bursting with pride at the sight of her titled employers.

Kartal steps forward to take photos of the four of us. It is an occasion filled with pomp and formality and I'd feel like an imposter except for the reassurance of Antal's warm hand on my back.

We head to the underground garage where Máté and Grigor await us, ready to open the doors of a town car. Its tinted windows mask us from onlookers although we can see out clearly. The car takes an exit at the rear of the parking area then follows a narrow lane through the back of the estate until we join the main road. This maneuver will trick anyone watching the Castle gates.

I still think it's insane of Antal to put himself at risk this way but he's certain the police will not dare effect an arrest in the Palace. Once the authorities see that we're accepted there they'll think twice before issuing an arrest warrant.

Again I remonstrate with him, hoping to have Csilla and Sándor's support. "Antal, you've told me that Hungary is a Republic so why do you think the police will hold back? it's not like they care about a Royal or rather an ex-Royal family."

Sándor dashes my hope of an ally when he intervenes to say: "Don't worry about this, Tó. There's no way the police would force their way into tonight's celebration. Even though they don't particularly like us shifters they respect the standing our wealth provides. And there will simply be too many high-profile guests in attendance as well as the inevitable *paparazzi* recording every detail."

Csilla leans forward to pat me with her gloved hand. "Besides Tó, if the police actually do show up with an arrest warrant Antal can shift and flee. There's no way they'd risk firing off guns in that crowd."

My mind immediately forms the image of Antal transforming into his dark gray wolf while leaving nothing behind but his white clothes. We'd all be left standing around in our finery watching the huge animal bound away with our mouths hanging open. The picture my imagination's conjured brings laughter bubbling up my throat and I can't contain my giggles.

Maybe I've communicated the image telepathically because instead of a reprimand Antal starts to chuckle as well. Csilla joins in as does Kartal so only Sándor is left to shake his head at our foolish behavior. . The privacy screen is up so Grigor and Máté won't have heard us, but I'm sure they'd laugh if they had.

Kartal gets out of the car as soon as we arrive at the Palace gates. He hands over the invitations and the barrier is lifted. A solider salutes us as we drive by.

I'm anxious about getting out of the backseat in this confection of a dress but Antal lifts me by the waist and murmuring *head down* slides me out of the car without mishap.

Voices call out and cameras flash as we're photographed by the crowd behind the barrier. I'm careful to maintain perfect posture and hold my head up. I gaze up at Antal who is looking down into my face so I give him a closed-mouth smile. I'm sure that will show a perfect picture of happy newlyweds.

The Palace looks straight out of a fairy-tale with a wide stone staircase, complete with red carpet, leading up to double doors that are thrown open. More uniformed soldiers stand guard while liveried servants hurry to guide us up the stairs and usher us inside. Several massive chandeliers light up the entrance and reflect in the many mirrors on the walls and on the checkerboard-tiled floor.

A butler-type in an elaborate costume adorned with miles of gold braid announces us. As his voice booms out the words *Her Royal Highness the Princess Lake* all the chatter stops. I can clearly hear waltz music played by an orchestra but every other sound is drowned out by the thunderous crashing in my ears. I realize it's the rush of blood from my pounding heart.

Prince River has never been a welcome sight until now. He steps forward wearing a quasi-military style of costume in aquamarine satin. It should look ridiculous but for some reason it suits him. There's a curvy platinum-blonde standing close beside him and I guess this is one of our cousins. I see a family resemblance.

River steps forward and taking hold of my hand by my gloved fingertips leads me towards the strangers who are our parents.

The reigning King and Queen of the Jagiellon don't smile or show any facial expression. For all their animation they could be carved from cold marble as they sit high on their thrones. Identical platinum hair color, pale skin, and the renowned aquamarine eyes all tell of generational inbreeding.

As I'm being introduced I can't suppress a shudder of loathing. When my gaze meets the narrowed eyes of my mother, the Queen, I see disgust, but the King shows a spark of interest in the beautiful young woman before him. My father is about to stand, perhaps to come forward in greeting, but the Queen halts him with a hand laid on his forearm. He immediately stills and for a moment the little family remains stiffly frozen.

My merest hint of a curtsy is blatantly discourteous, and when I hear Csilla's agonized groan I realize my ears are working again. The Queen's mouth purses in disapproval before she casts her eyes beyond me, her estranged daughter, to the next guest.

With my head held high, floating in the gorgeous gown, I move on, my eyes glancing at the people who bow murmuring *Princess Lake* without acknowledging their words.

River returns me to Antal and I don't bother to hide my smirk when he says in a low voice: "That looked like fun." A sharp laugh escapes me and I share a genuine smile with my husband. We are a confident, stunning couple with him so tall, handsome and masculine, and me with my pale coloring glittering in the shimmering of the diamante studs sewn into this ballgown. We are a spectacle dazzling the onlookers and stealing everyone's attention.

"Husband," I say quietly, forcing Antal to dip his head so he can hear me. "Husband, I'm so glad this dress has layers upon layers of gauze and silk otherwise everyone would see just how hungry my poor pussy is for my mate's big dick."

His only reaction is a slight tightening of the skin around his eyes as his gaze meets mine. His eyes are bright and burning with the promise of retribution. That look sears right through me and I shiver in anticipation.

"Yes, it's such a needy, greedy little pussy... all swollen and tender," I continue without shame. "A few tears escaped before, but now it's crying freely. I think the wet has traveled the whole way down my leg right into my shoes."

The arm holding mine gives an involuntary jerk and I thrill in my power. I'm pretending my desire is just another tedious ordeal I have to get through. With a deep sigh I whisper that *I'm aching, that the need to feel my husband's hard cock splitting me open and ruthlessly pounding my slick passage is all I can think about.* Antal picks up the pace and our leisurely stroll has now turned into a march.

After promenading a circuit through the great hall, greeting the few people Antal knows, we arrive once again before the Highnesses.

Completely breaking protocol I speak first. In a clear voice I announce: "Your Highnesses, I am taking this stately occasion to renounce my title of Princess and to relinquish any claim on this Royal Family. Good evening, and we needn't meet again."

Antal's chest inflates with pride thinking *how regal my wife is as she looks each of her parents square in the face then gracefully turns away.* Re-taking my arm he leads us out of the hall forcing himself to maintain an unhurried pace.

Even the musicians have paused to watch so the rustling noise made by the dipping and swaying of my gown is the only sound in the huge room.

As we walk down the wide stone stair Antal whispers his promise of a thorough punishing fuck. Kartal will have to arrange a different ride home for his Alpha because we're taking the car.

A Princess No More

Tó

Lying in bed that night a kaleidoscope of faces runs through my mind. I can't put names to most of them but their images remain. Expressions range from avid curiosity to polite interest, from outright anger to cool disdain.

I would never have felt like part of that Court, I think. *I wasn't welcome, and I didn't exactly send out friendly vibes myself. I had way more fun at the Castle work party than I did at our visit to the Palace.*

Relieved and glad to put the dreaded, stuffy occasion behind us I cling to Antal in the back of the limo. Well, to his arm because all the stiff layers of my ballgown prevent me from getting closer. We are the first ones back at the Castle, and with a happy sigh Antal comments *it's good to be here again.*

Ladiszla greets us with a curtsy saying she'll *send up a maid to help Princess Lake with her dress.* The idea of me being Royalty has a magical effect on the cranky old servant.

I figure I might as well get it over with and start updating people on my change in status. "Thank you Ladiszla, but I'm no longer a princess so I don't need help."

Antal and I hurry up to our suite before Ladiszla can recover from the shock and demand answers to her questions.

Now that we're in the privacy of our bedroom Antal lifts me onto the high mattress and gathering up all the layers and layers of tulle he drags them up covering my head. Laughing I grab hold of the fabric, pressing it down, so I can peek over at my husband. He is entranced at the sight

159

of my naked body under the *virginal debutante* gown. I felt wickedly delicious with the knowledge the whole time we were out.

With the back of the dress bunched up and raising my hips I present my pussy, prettily pink and swollen with arousal, like an offering. Antal accepts the invitation with a probing tongue that pushes in deep before pulling back to swirl around my clit. He grasps a fistful of buttock to hold me steady while the other hand slips through my satiny folds and his fingers curl to prod my g-spot. I can't help the tremble in my legs at the electrifying sensations inside and out.

Antal doesn't let up on his oral assault merely chuckling when I shimmy and beg beneath his fingers and mouth. He laps up my wetness with loud slurps saying *mmm-mmm* like I'm the most delicious flavor his tastebuds have ever encountered. I'm mortified and entranced by the salacious sounds. Teasing me mercilessly Antal now nibbles on my protruding clit until I'm is crying and pleading for release *Antal please, please, I need to cum please!*

"Maybe it wasn't so smart to act the cocktease, hmm wife?"

Gasping out the words I exclaim: "That wasn't teasing, that was just a bit of fun–"

"Or maybe you weren't acting? Maybe that's all you really are, eh? Just a bratty, naughty cocktease who chose to play with the wrong man."

I know my pleasure is merely a second or two away but once again Antal pulls back. In a frustration of temper I scream and drum my heels on the bed but my husband simply laughs at my tantrum before getting up and leaving me spread and exposed. Antal removes his sash and the jacket of his tuxedo. I watch hungrily as he unbuttons his white shirt to reveal the dark skin of his hairy, tattooed chest.

Reaching in his pocket he finds his phone and makes a call. I give him an angry look but he silences my whiny complaint with a glare.

"Grigor? Come to my room now, I need my Beta to provide some much-needed discipline to my naughty Omega."

I feel my eyes widen in a mixture of shock and fear. I know that among Grigor's duties one of the most important is disciplining wayward she-wolves with corporal punishment. But surely not tonight? Antal won't subject his mate to the painful humiliation of a spanking by his Beta, will he? A spanking, huh! I've seen the results of Grigor's handiwork still coloring Maritzsa's bottom for hours afterwards.

Not a minute later there's a firm knock on the door and Antal motions Grigor inside.

I've pushed down my dress as best I can but Grigor barely gives me a glance before taking hold of an ankle and dragging me down to the edge of the bed. Reams of crinoline bunch then spring back as I put up a useless fight. If I wasn't so worried about what's coming I'd find the whole episode comical.

In a flash I'm neatly trapped across the Beta's wide, muscular thigh with my hands pinned behind my back with my bottom bared and vulnerable. Grigor corrals the gauzy layers and pushes them down to blanket my head and upper body. I can't see a thing but I can hear the men's conversation.

In a very matter-of-fact manner Grigor says: "Alpha, I never expected to be correcting your mate so the Omega must have committed a very serious infraction. How severely do you want her punished?"

"Not at all!" I shout, frantic to avoid his heavy hand and the subsequent embarrassment. I've swallowed this man's cock, I've licked his ball-sack,

I've begged him to fuck me when I've been in heat but this is something else altogether. How will I ever face him again?

Both of them ignore me as Antal coldly replies: "Treat her as if she's the newest maid in the household and you've just caught her trying to hide the shattered remains of an expensive vase, and lying about who broke it. I will tell you when to stop."

Grigor's huge hand begins beating down in sharp smacks. I thought that out of affection for me he might hold back some of his strength but no, not at all! I still can't see a thing through this damn dress but I sure can feel. His hard palm delivers stinging spanks that soon have me sobbing in pain and writhing to escape.

"Not such a mouthy tease now, are you wife?"

"Antal I'm sorry! I'm so sorry I didn't realize... I never meant... OWWWW!" I end on a howl as Grigor's heavy hand has smacked its way down to my tender sit spot.

"Look at you wriggling like a hooked worm! And you're cute ass is turning so red! What a show you're putting on for me. Grigor, why haven't we done this before?" questions Antal with a delighted laugh.

Now I'm glad my face is hidden because I know it burns in shame to match my flaming bum. Antal's enjoyment of my humiliating predicament makes the punishment a thousand times worse.

"You've never been interested in spankings like this, Alpha. You only use the whip or the flogger because Tó won't let you use that paddle with the embedded nails so–"

"Oh I wouldn't call them nails, more like tacks... and just little tacks, at that..."

I hear him pause and I know he's picturing my poor ass being subjected to that horrific paddle. My *noooo!* is muffled but I'm certain he can hear me, even if he ignores me and pretends otherwise.

"I always thought mere hand spanking was way too vanilla but my God man, you've got her *kövér alján [plump bottom]* glowing! When did Tó grow out of her tiny, skinny ass into this? Look how she jiggles when she squirms and tries to fight... so fucking hot!"

"You're feeling that because she's your mate. There's nothing arousing for me in disciplining this Omega, it's simply my duty. I'm sure you'll experience deep pleasure if I move her onto your lap and leave you two to it." Grigor's hinting isn't the least bit subtle.

Mesmerized by the sight of my shimmying red backside Antal nods. Grigor has really done a number on me. Now he easily lifts me, still bent over from the weight of the gown, and places my helpless body across my husband's lap. Antal lays his palm gently over my hot flesh and I can feel his cock harden even more as I wriggle against it. Grigor leaves, closing the door with a slight slam.

"Only the most *buta feleség [foolish wife]* publicly taunts her *kegyetlen férj [cruel husband]*, especially when he's a man as *ördögi [vicious]* as me," Antal announces laying down a fusillade of painful swats on my poor, throbbing bottom. "Are you a *bocsánat kislány [sorry little girl]* now?"

"Oh yes, I am I'm so sorry. Antal please STOP! I'm sorry, sorry, sorry, and I'll never do it again–"

Antal gives me a couple of gentler strokes but tells me *it's fascinating how your flesh ripples on impact like it's inviting me to deliver much firmer spanks.*

"Tó, *olyan szép vagy [you are so beautiful]* over my knee. Your pretty *piros mögött [red behind]* is exquisite. I can smell your enticing, horny scent and it excites me."

Pausing to slip his fingers between my rosy cheeks Antal chuckles at the wet evidence of his wife's arousal from being punished by her fated mate. "Oh I think we're both going to look forward to me giving you lots of real spankings, not just the one-two smacks you get now."

After several more minutes of shame and pain Antal stops and flips me onto the bed. Gravity still holds the dress down over my head when he lifts me up on my knees in the doggie-style position. Antal says he admires *the delectable sight of your well-spanked bum and swollen pussy* and I can just picture my rosy flesh as it emerges from a sea of frothy white fabric.

Growling his approval he lines up his cock and rubs up and down against my slick opening. Antal's teasing send tremors to my core and when he presses his thumbs against my vulnerable butt-hole I buck my hips in a wanton plea to be fucked. He can't hear the actual words I say, they're deadened by all the layers of cloth, but my meaning is shamelessly clear.

At this moment I'm reduced to nothing more than a pleading Omega beseeching her Alpha to take what's his.

I didn't know that bit of skin between my two holes is so sensitive until he presses down, curving his fingertips into my butt-hole. When he massages there an electric sensation goes straight to my core. Even my nipples feel the zing. It makes me cry out *more-more-more PLEASE!*

Antal spreads my thighs and holding my hips he plunges all the way in then almost all the way out in a steady rhythmic stroke. I work my pelvis to add friction. My inner walls clutch tightly at him when he withdraws then relax to invite him back in. His two fingers up inside my tight rear give me an overwhelming sensation of fullness.

The pulsations throb along his cock and I seem him grit his teeth as his knot grows, moving along his shaft. I flinch when his free hand clutches my tender butt-cheeks and cry out when I'm breached. The edging from earlier makes me explode and Antal joins me in a ball-draining blast. We're tied together in profound intimacy and Antal burrows through all the material of the dress until he can find my face for a kiss. I turn my head to catch his mouth and now we're fused together in two ways.

My ass is burning and my pussy is aching too, I think, as I snuggle against Antal's broad chest. Everything from my waist down is so sore that I silently resolve *never to tease him like that again.*

I don't want any more spankings because it's affected me emotionally in an unpleasant way. Being chastised like a naughty child makes me feel small, a debilitating angst I thought I'd left in my past. This is distinctly different from Antal's usual violence. Physically it's far less damaging but emotionally? it's devastating.

Unfortunately it feeds my Omega need to submit to my Alpha. The heated skin of my butt is nothing compared to the fire he kindled in my core. I've never felt such a desperate longing to be fucked outside of a heat.

When he wields an impact implement forcefully enough to bruise and welt me I know he's exorcizing his evil impulses. It hurts a lot. But in my adolescence I learned how to retreat into my mind, distancing myself from the physical pain of cold, hunger, and beatings. In my mind I call it a fugue state although I'm not sure if that's the right term.

Antal's savagery frequently draws blood and the sight always excites him. He even finds his own bloodletting a turn-on. I've become skillful in weighing just the right pressure to employ when dragging a knife or the nasty spiked wheel against his skin.

I'm never ashamed when Antal licks the blood – mine or his – off my body. That never touches my sensibility or self-esteem, not the way that demeaning spanking did.

But I have to admit... already I regret how the sharpness of the sting has dulled, and how I miss being left wet and wanting. The humiliation does add a filip of spice to being dominated by my Alpha.

Oh! that must be it... Grigor said spanking acts as an aphrodisiac for fated mates. And corporal punishment is the approved disciplinary practice of the pack.

My mind continues flashing photos in my head. Images of the people and the decor at the Palace this evening are interspersed with a picture of naked limbs entwined on sweaty, bloody sheets in a dimly lit bedroom reeking of sex.

Gradually the ache in my body eases and my mind clears so I can drift into a light sleep.

Antal

Something about the elegant perfection of my icy blonde ignites a desire from deep within me to smash and destroy. The conundrum is why I feel pride at the sight of Tó with her hair piled up, her chin held high, dressed in a fairy-tale ballgown at the same time as wanting to knock her down and hold her with my foot pinning that exquisite neck to wallow in the muck. I suspect it's my kink but maybe it's also hers? Maybe it's her demon surfacing to call out mine?

When we got back I was ready to reward her teasing with a good hard fucking but once I realized that underneath her gown she'd been naked all night I was overcome by the urge to demean and punish my classy-looking princess.

Her dress is ruined by stains and rips but my Tó is satiated and the beast inside me is tamed... for now.

After a lengthy interval of dozy comfort luxuriating in the haze of our knotting, I slowly pull out of my wife's perfect cunt. *So much cum,* I think, *both mine and hers spilling out of her luscious holes.* Semen runs down Tó's thighs and I gather the moisture into my hands like it's massage oil that I smooth back over her tender, well-used flesh.

Mine, mine, mine I hum to myself. She lazily opens her beautiful eyes and the two of us communicate our feelings without words.

The next morning I hold Tó cuddled in my lap while I skim through the news on the iPad. She wiggles her ass trying to harden my cock but I'm engrossed in the item I'm reading. Her lips latch onto my nipple and she sucks the cotton of my t-shirt into her mouth wetting the fabric and lightly biting down. It's a risky move because I'll just dump her ass to the floor if I'm irritated.

Instead I pull back and looking down see Tó with her half-lidded eyes and moist, parted lips gazing back. I've been fighting my own arousal at the feel of her soft, squirming bottom but lose the battle when faced with this lustful longing. Naughty wife!

Exhaling a fake exasperated sigh I tell her: "When I finish this article you can suck my cock."

Tó tilts her head and impertinently asks: "Is it a *looooong* article?"

I learned how to school my facial expressions years ago but the stern line of my lips is belied by the twinkle in my eye. "I will read it out loud," I proclaim and then do so:

"Princess Lake is a *Princess No More* according to an official announcement issued last night. Eyebrows are raised at the surprisingly late hour for a Palace communication – almost as if they were rushing it into circulation? We've included the full release at the end of our report.

We can't help being the teeniest bit suspicious at how this dovetails with the police dropping the accusation of murder against her husband. Isn't that timing just a little suspect? EuroVibes has more questions:

Did Princess Lake truly make this decision on her own?

Was the murder charge faked in order to force her co-operation?

Is our beautiful Princess once again a pawn in Royal machinations?

The public demands answers! and EuroVibes seeks out the TRUTH!"

"Oh those foolish people trying to fan the flames of a non-existent scandal!" exclaims an indignant Tó.

"What they're doing is building up readership, followers I think they call it, and they've found an audience eager to believe in cover-ups, conspiracies, and secret agendas."

"I don't like how they've made it sound like you're guilty but got saved by a deal. That's not how it is at all."

"No, and now it makes it even more important to prove my case."

"And then all this will stop?"

Lifting Tó off my lap and onto her knees on the floor I open my pants and fist my cock. Although Tó huffs in annoyance I'm well aware that giving me a blowjob is one of her favorite things.

She once told me she thinks my dick is ugly, always angry-looking and veiny, but that she loves to make her man lose control. I think I hate that part. Dominance flows through my veins just as surely as my blood does. I don't cave in or let loose easily.

When we first got together I would pull her off just in time to spray cum all over her face and chest. As Tó learned to take me deeper I started shooting down her throat when I'd stuffed her so full she struggled to take in air.

She would lock her streaming eyes with mine and her triumph at the sight of my face screwed up in pleasure was near-orgasmic. Tó explained it isn't the power that overwhelms her, it's because I'm giving her my trust. My vulnerability.

Tó obediently opens her mouth but before wrapping me in her hot lips she looks up waiting for an answer.

Pushing her into position I chuckle saying: "*Édes baba [sweet baby]*, so naive. It will be replaced by other gossip but won't ever stop. Every time the Royal Family hits the headlines a paragraph or two about *the shameful secret of Princess Lake* will be included."

Rapidly running her flattened tongue along the big vein in my cock Tó grins evilly and says: "Good!" before swallowing deep and working her mouth.

Tó

Meeting up with Csilla and Sándor for a late breakfast Antal and I hear all about what happened after we left the Palace last night.

"That was quite a bombshell you dropped!" exclaims Sándor in a wondering tone.

Csilla gleefully adds: "No one could talk about anything else! And it's funny because well, obviously they didn't want you, Erzsébet told us how jealous they all are of each other so a newcomer would never be welcome, but now that you've turned your back on them suddenly they all *wished they knew you better*. It's all so hypocritical and such nasty, back-biting gossip!" She gives a mock shudder which makes us all laugh.

"Food was served but frankly you didn't miss much. It was a disappointing spread, and I suspect that was the Queen's doing."

"I probably should have guessed that my renunciation would cause a bit of a media frenzy but it's actually turned out much worse. We know that the palace eagerly accepted my abdication but it seems the *social justice warriors* think it's all a con!"

"What?"

"Yeah, these Internet news sites are full of theories about coercion and stuff. Anyhow, we were thinking that another post from Erzsébet might help quash the conspiracy theory. What do you think?"

"Let me get them on a video call. Just give me a moment and... good morning, Janos. As you can see we're all gathered round the table eating, as usual, yes, and Tó would like a word with Erzsébet if she's there?"

Erzsébet's face appears and this morning her complexion is rosy with no signs of sickness at all. She looks great. I explain the predicament and ask if Erzsébet thinks another post will do any good.

"Oh, I don't know but maybe... Do I say that I know you? My original post was under an assumed identity. Same as yesterday's."

"I think this time the truth is best. We need to fight this implication that me stepping down is the price of having the charges against Antal stayed. That's just wrong. He deserves to be publicly vindicated."

"Oh that opens up an interesting angle..." Erzsébet muses. She thinks for a moment then her face lights up with a wicked grin. "I've got it! Right now it looks like you guys made a deal in Antal's favor but what if we turn that story upside-down and imply you were coerced into giving up your title or they'd throw Antal in jail? You know, something like *Royals threaten: lose the crown or lose your husband* that sort of thing. Make him the victim instead of the winner, and make Tós renunciation a huge sacrifice for the love of her life. After all, the best way to fight a conspiracy is with a bigger conspiracy."

I turn to Antal asking: "What do you think?"

"I think I'd be a lousy husband if I let you give it all up for me."

"I understand what Antal means. Okay so the best, in fact the only, way to do this right is to prove who really killed Kada," puts in Sándor.

"Oh I think we're all in agreement that it must have been Beáta, right?" I state.

Csilla and Erzsébet exchange a wordless communication before Csilla announces: "We women will pay Beáta a visit."

Extracting a Confession

Tó

Once again Máté is driving us to the Erdős home. We've detoured to pick up Erzsébet who made it quite clear that she isn't going to be left out of this confrontation. *Of course she won't, controversy is her middle name!* I think, glad she's on our side.

We're all pumped up with the excitement of real-life sleuthing but haven't planned how we'll handle it. I figure Csilla will start off being courteous and reasonable, then Erzsébet will jump in with a challenge or a demand, leaving me to attack whatever Beáta says.

Erzsébet isn't the only one hoping for a fight. Beáta has threatened my husband and I can't – I won't – back down. She's a low-down lying bitch making a vicious accusation. Beáta Szémozsa is my enemy.

Those three have known each other since they were teenagers and it sounds like they were never friends as girls or now as women. Csilla decided not to call ahead and we can see the surprise, quickly followed by a scowl, on Beáta's face when she answers the door.

"Well, well look who's descended on me. I'd never have expected you ladies to make a condolence call," she smirks.

"Are we going to have this conversation on the porch with your neighbors listening? or are you going to invite us in?" Csilla speaks in an even tone but her words carry a hint of threat. Beáta replies by stepping back from the doorway and with a wide, mocking gesture ushers us inside.

The foyer is stylish, but cold and uninspired. Matte tiles in several shades of gray cover the floor and one wall. Another holds a massive mirror, almost floor-to-ceiling high. It isn't mirrored closet doors, it's solid glass in a heavy frame and it must weigh a ton. *That would have been a bitch to hang,* I speculate to myself.

We follow our reluctant hostess into a formal reception room. The furniture is that spindly style, French I think, upholstered in gold and blue brocade, the carpet patterned but insipidly pale-colored, and the only wall decoration is a tapestry that was probably chosen because it fits the color scheme.

Motioning us towards the uncomfortable chairs Beáta seats herself on a matching loveseat. It's obvious she won't be offering refreshments.

Csilla does open the conversation but what she says is unexpected: "Beáta you're right in supposing we're not here to commiserate with you over the death of your husband. We know you hated him, we know you killed him. We're here to demand you exonerate Antal."

Beáta's eyes widen and then an angry flush rises up from her chest joining the high color in her cheeks. She looks angry and belligerent snapping: "You can't prove a thing."

"We don't even want to try. We're hear for your confession, that's all we need."

"Ha! As if I'm going to confide anything in you two," then turning to me she adds: "And I don't even know who you are—"

"You know perfectly well this is Antal's wife Tó," replies Csilla.

"Ah, the so-called princess, am I right?"

"Ex-princess," I reply coolly. "I renounced the title of Princess Lake. Last night, as a matter of fact."

"So the rumors really were true? about you with those eyes being Shifter Royalty? and now you're married to Antal? Huh! Kada will be spinning in his grave from jealousy!"

She cackles a mean laugh until Erzsébet jumps in saying: "Don't fuck us around, Beáta. You've made a lot of trouble and now you've got to fix it."

"Excuse me but I don't *have* to do anything. I don't care who you think you are Erzsébet Erdős–"

"Oh I'll tell you exactly who I am–"

"STOP!" I shout over them. "Mrs. Szémozsa, hmm that's stupid, I'm a Mrs. Szémozsa, too. Okay I'm just going to call you Beáta since we're sister-in-laws or is it sisters-in-law?" They all shut up when I yelled and now that I'm rambling over semantics I'm getting puzzled looks. I better get to the point. "Beáta you look like you could use a drink, in fact you look hungover and probably need an alcoholic pick-me-up."

"I'd love one, but I can't," she replies sullenly. "I'm waiting for the police right now. I called them to come and take a new statement so that means I have to be sober. In fact when you rang the doorbell I thought you were them."

Csilla moves to sit beside Beáta covering the widow's hand with her own. "Tell us what happened," she says with compassion. Beáta looks at her closely and sees nothing but sincerity. Her own eyes well up with tears as she tells us her story.

"I don't know, not exactly. I realized I'd drank too much and said way too much to Imre... That's why I phoned that detective and told him I'm withdrawing my statement. I explained that I was too muddled with grief and shock to know what I was saying. And actually that part is true... well except for the grief, I mean you know... I'm still not really clear what did happen, but this time I fought back and Kada... Kada died."

"Kada attacked you," I say as a statement, not a question.

"Yes. He was angry and he took it out on me."

"And not for the first time either, right?"

Beáta shakes her head and her eyes fill up again. She's bottled her secrets and her feelings for far too long and now she longs to tell the truth. Ignoring Erzsébet she turns from Csilla to me and tells us what she remembers from that night.

"I didn't mean to kill him, I just wanted to stop him long enough so I could get away. Not away, away but just out of the room to escape from him and his anger.

See he'd knocked me to the ground and as I scrambled towards the hallway I used the doorstep for balance and I p-pulled it up-up w-with me and swung..." now the tears stream and her voice is choked with sobs. Csilla pats the woman's back in a soothing gesture.

Neither Erzsébet nor I am moved by Beáta's waterworks but we both recognize a crying jag when we hear one. All we can do is wait her out. After accepting tissues from Csilla Beáta draws a deep breath, dabs at her eyes and blows her nose. Then she turns her watery gaze to me.

"I never meant to hurt Antal and I don't know why I even mentioned him." She's full of shit and my thoughts must show because she hurries on with her theory that Antal must have been on her mind. That it was a shock to see him at the party. "It's been years and years since I saw him."

I'm sure my expression is stony and obviously not buying her excuse but before I can respond Erzsébet says: "What have you said to the police now?"

"I admitted that Antal wasn't there, and I was mixed-up. I said I was terrified that my husband would kill me but I never meant for him to die."

"So you did confess to killing Kada?"

"Yes, but in self-defense."

"You need a lawyer."

"I've already got one. She's on her way over here as well. She says I'm not to sign anything until she can look it over."

"No matter what the Szémozsa pack might have thought about Kada they won't want you any more," states Erzsébet bluntly.

Beáta huffs a laugh saying: "Any more? They never wanted me in the first place. You're right, I have no home with them. I want to return to my human family. My only way forward is to confess and throw myself on the mercy of the court."

"And being human you'll have a huge advantage doing that. You can stoke up the prejudices about feral shifters coming after human women and treating them cruelly." Erzsébet's disdain is evident in her tone.

Beáta has regained her composure and now she just shrugs saying, "Well in my case that's exactly what happened."

I stand up, suddenly desperate to get out of here and away from this noxious woman. "Lie all you like so long as you clear Antal's name," I tell her as I move towards the front door.

Erzsébet follows me muttering *human bitch!* loudly enough for Beáta to hear.

Csilla gets up as well firing off a parting shot: "Know that Imre taped your conversation so your confession is on record and I have a copy of the file."

We leave the house while Beáta fumes: "That's not legal."

"No, but damning nevertheless."

Máté has moved the town car from the driveway to the road, making room for a late model BMW. As we walk to our ride we watch an expensive-looking professional woman, middle-aged, get out of the Beemer.

Her gray hair is perfectly styled and she wears red-framed glasses that match her lipstick, her nails, and the soles of her designer shoes. Beáta has hired herself a very pricey attorney. She stares openly at us but we don't engage.

Climbing through the car door that Máté holds open we just get settled when a police car pulls up. As we drive past we can see sour looks as the two detectives step out and greet the lawyer.

"Ugh! I need to get rid of this nasty taste in my mouth after listening to that miserable bitch," exclaims Erzsébet.

"Come home with us and we'll have something to eat and drink while we let the men know what's happened. If Janos can't join us Máté will drive you home after."

"Thanks, Csilla. I'll call my husband now and he'll meet us at your place."

Csilla smiles at me saying: "I'm so glad Beáta confessed and Antal won't be arrested. I don't even know if Beáta will be, or if the *államügyész*, um, attorney general? no, it's district attorney. I don't know if the district attorney will pursue the case or not, but we'll make sure word gets out to the media and the social media," she adds with a nod at Erzsébet.

"There is something I don't understand," I begin but stop, feeling hesitant. The two women look at me with a question on their faces so I continue but first explain: "Maybe this is intrusive but... I wondered why you all fell out and why Beáta is such an unhappy woman. I mean, I can tell she's a drinker and it's not a new vice but..."

Csilla nods at Erzsébet who tells me: "The answer to both your questions is the same and that is it's Beáta's nature. Even as a girl nothing was ever good enough for her. Despite being the prettiest, she was never satisfied with what she had. She wanted the most expensive clothes, the latest gadgets, the best of everything. And, of course, it didn't take long for her to realize she chose the wrong brother.

I suspect her drinking began early on in the marriage because Kada never stopped playing the field. His lack of respect shamed her and his lack of love embittered her."

"Oh Erzsébet you put that so well. That's exactly how it is with Beáta, and her sour disposition drove all her friends away. Not that she really had friends. She was suspicious of females and males were suspicious of her," Csilla muses.

"Her poor choices worked out the best though because she would have made Antal miserable. Between her jealousy and dissatisfaction she would have dragged him down and frankly everyone knows there is a black despair inside him already."

Turning to me she smiles adding: "We've all seen how much lighter and happier he is with you in his life, Tó."

I've seen a change in him myself.

Arriving back at the Castle we share our good news with the men and then Gyuri comes over with both Réka and Marta and several other couples arrive so it turns into another impromptu party. I don't know if it's a Hungarian thing, or a European thing, or a shifter thing, but this crowd turns every happy occasion into a festive celebration.

Everyone is excited to meet me, ostensibly as Antal's wife, but truly because of my Royal blood. I repeatedly have to remind them that I'm an ex-princess.

We all drink Pálinka except for Erzsébet who is avoiding alchohol and indulging her pregnancy craving for chocolate milk. I notice that Antal is also mindful of his consumption, no doubt remembering the recent hangover he suffered.

I don't drink much either, never having had the chance to acquire a taste for liquor. I quite like champagne, though. The bubbles are fun, and it's a quick, easy way to get pleasantly light-headed.

My Alpha sends me a wave of lust and thoughts of steamy sex push drinking out of my mind. Meeting his hot gaze I give him a slow smile of compliance. Antal reaches for my hand and with a loud *Goodnight, everyone. We're still on our honeymoon*, he leads me away. I hear the guests calling out *congratulations* and *time to celebrate*.

As soon as we leave the room Antal scoops me up in his arms. I'm used to him carrying me around and sitting me on his knee at home, but I don't expect it here where we're among friendly strangers. Well, more than strangers... I'm forming real friendships, and Antal is reconnecting with his family.

My thoughts scatter as I feel Antal's laser focus on me. Before losing myself in the depths of his dark eyes I make a silly comment: "I'm getting too heavy to carry around... you've fed me too well."

He snorts in denial adding "You are rounder now. I like it. No more seeing each rib, or being poked by your hip bone. Even your knobby spine is hidden from me now. Tó is my *szexi feleség [sexy wife]* and you will never be too heavy for me to carry."

Something in his face stops me from the joke I'm about to make. I look more closely trying to put a name to what I'm seeing. Antal looks curious and happy and... and loving. He leans in and gives me the gentlest, most tender kiss ever. The feeling it instills makes me want to cry but I shake off such a foolish thought.

"Everything is different now, isn't it?"

I can only nod, speech having deserted me in the wake of all this emotion.

He nods back, understanding why I'm mute. "Yes," he says and that one word says it all. Somehow we've transcended from what we were to something new and wonderful and scary. I no longer feel like we're a match made in hell. Although it sure as shit isn't the least bit heavenly. Especially when he lowers his mouth to whisper in my ear:

"I miss my knives, Tó. It didn't feel right to bring them to someone else's home because... well, because of the mess. I can't wait until we're back in our own bed so I can play and play and hear you scream."

Aaaaand there he is, I think.

A Scandal For Christmas

Antal

Our private celebration is an incredibly dirty, soaking mess of semen and sweat. I can't stop producing seed and have jetted ropes of cum over Tó's face, her tits, and her ass. An ass that's still showing pink from last night's spanking. She attacked my body with all the fever of an Omega heat and we both battled to overpower the other. I took her in a variety of positions but each time I held her down she'd squirm her way back on top of me. I loved every fucking minute of it.

We began with me stating I wanted to give her a close physical inspection. There's a small dining-area in our suite so I told her to strip and lay down on the table with her legs wide apart. Tó's nipples turned to hard points before I even laid a finger on her.

Bending down to her chest I say *hmmm* as I palpate her tits. I feel the slight swell of her breast as I roll the palm of my hand back and forth across her nipples. "Your tits have grown bigger... rounder. Your nipples are a healthy, inviting color," I add as I nip first one then the other between my teeth and strum them with the tip of my tongue. Tó groans with pleasure. Reaching across to hold a tit in each hand I massage in a circular motion, pausing to squeeze the flesh in my fingers. The rise and fall of her chest quickens with her loudly exhaled breaths. I inspect the sides leaving a trail of goosebumps and with a hand at her back to lift her torso I cup each breast and jiggle it to feel the weight.

"Absolutely perfect," I declare, before moving down to her belly. Tó has now propped herself up on her elbows so she can watch what I'm doing.

Her stomach is still flat but the skin is soft and smooth. If I keep feeding her rich foods she's grown to love she will develop a little roundness to her belly. I dip my finger inside her navel, an *innie*, but she pulls my hand away saying *ewww*.

"What's wrong?"

"I don't like the way that feels, I don't even touch it myself."

Dropping my face down I fill the little indent with my tongue asking: "How's that?"

She considers a moment before saying: "Better, definitely better but it still feels tickly or tingly or something."

Keeping my mouth on her flesh I move down trailing kisses. Tó's pubic hair is white-blonde and only sparsely covers her mound. I comb out the few strands with my fingers then tug hard. She squeals and giggles. The tuft of hair stops above her clitoris and none grows on the side of her pussy so her pretty pink cunt is bare and fully exposed without needing to be shaved or waxed. For a moment I'm distracted, speculating how a bare cunt would look on a she-wolf.

My fingers are gentle as I prod and poke my way through this examination and from her involuntary twitches I know her body yearns for a firmer touch. I peel back her labia and lean in close to study, sniff, and lick. Her pussy pulsates as she flexes.

"Congratulations Mrs. Szémozsa, the look, smell, and taste indicates you have a perfectly healthy cunt."

Her eyes glitter under lowered lids as she spreads her thighs wider and tells me: "Then go ahead and use it as it should be used, Mr. Szémozsa."

"Oh I will, but first there's this little puckered rosebud to unfurl."

She gasps when I tap her butt-hole with the pad of my finger but lifts her hips to give me easier access. I push in up to my first knuckle and wiggling the tip of my finger feel her heat. There's a sheen to her pussy lips and I breathe in the scent of her arousal.

Lifting her up I sit her on the very edge of the table. Her legs dangle down until I take hold of her feet and place them flat on the wooden surface. Now she's wide open and primed so I quickly push down my pants and pull her onto my cock.

I reach behind to cup both ass cheeks to cushion each bump up and down on the hard table. Her head is thrown back and I can see her throat pulsing rapidly. I'm fascinated by the way her little tits bounce, every part of her body is in motion.

Tó brings her face forward and looks down to watch where we're joined. I follow the direction of her gaze and see my cock sliding in and out, in and out, shiny with slick and pre-cum. I feel the muscles in my butt tighten.

Spinning us around I'm now the one using the table for support while she clings to me like a monkey with her legs wrapped tightly around my waist. She cums with a high-pitched mewling sound while I growl out through clenched teeth. I love the sounds she makes.

Eventually my breath slows enough that I can speak again. I remember being a young man and asking an older friend what's the best fuck you ever had? and I've never forgotten his answer. He said it's the next one. I realized then that sex should always be approached with optimism for the sheer joy of the act.

Flopping down on the bed I tell her she passed her physical and she playfully smacks my chest saying: "I should inspect you now."

"You could try but right now there's nothing to see," I explain since my cock in now tucked back inside its foreskin.

"Is being uncircumcised an age thing? like at the time when you were born hospitals didn't do it?"

That makes me laugh. "Tó, think about it... it's not an age thing it's a shifter thing. Can you imagine my wolf cock just hanging out all the time? How would I run? how would I fight?

It's funny but I was just thinking the same thing about you, I mean if you had your pussy waxed." I hug her tight to my chest still chuckling as I think *I have to remember to tell Grigor!*

Things have changed between us. Claiming her publicly through marriage is part of it but I know the real watershed moment was our knotting. Tó is mine, all mine, only mine, always mine.

A long time ago I discovered, in my work as an interrogator for our enterprise, that sexual pleasure can also be derived from screams of pain. I learned that whenever a session of intensive questioning drew to its inevitable close I'd be desperate to finish the job so I could go find a woman to fuck.

I'd be too hard to waste time cleaning myself up first. Instead, I'd shove my blood-splattered body between a female's spread thighs and rut into her. Grigor is in charge of my staff and he always made sure the girls were compensated after I used them.

He told me most were willing to meet me in my bed if I wanted more. I found that most women enjoy being roughly manhandled so long as there's plenty of passion and not just brutality.

All of that changed when I brought Tó home from that club where they worked her and treated her like a dog.

Tó plays with my demon in ways no one ever has before. She satisfies him like no one else ever could. She lays him to rest for ever-longer periods at a time.

"Now that Kada's gone I like being around my family and friends again. Do you want to settle here? Would you like to stay?"

"Here? In Hungary?" Tó's mouth hangs open in surprise and her reaction puzzles me.

"Yes, here in Hungary, you and me."

"And not go back to the States?"

Ah, now I'm the one who is surprised. "Living there means that much to you?"

She stops herself from uttering a quick reply and I can see the thoughts going round and round in her brain from the expressions chasing across her face.

Speaking slowly she finally says: "No, no it doesn't, but... it's the only place I've known. I've always been an American even though I've recently learned I'm not, or at least not American-born. I definitely feel way more American than Hungarian. I mean it's nice here and everything but it's all strange to me."

Tó, my tough *kis harcos [little warrior]*, is struggling to hide her emotion because she hates letting anyone see her cry. Even when my demon self is punishing her flesh she tries so hard to hold back her tears.

She confessed once that she's worried I'll think she's weak but I will never think that. No, she is my *bátor kislány [brave girl]*, my *kis hős [little hero]*.

Tő's tears intrigue me. They signal that her body is in pain or her feelings are in turmoil. Her body I can soothe with sex, but I don't really understand her feelings so... I suspect I'm not much good at comfort. I think she prefers my indifference anyhow.

However we do need to take some time and figure out where we should live.

I make a good living in America, we have a nice home, the weather is great all year long, and we're comfortable there. On the other hand here in Hungary I have my pack, my family, friends, familiar places, familiar food – I stop, realizing what's familiar to me is strange to Tő. That's what's making her so hesitant.

"You've never had the chance to experience pack life and I think you'll love it. There isn't much to figure out, it will just feel right."

"I... I don't really know how to say this but," she breaks off with annoyed huff. I remain silent, waiting for her to find the right words.

Finally she lifts her chin with a defiant air saying: "I don't like the idea of sharing you. I want us to live together in our own little bubble, just the two of us. Otherwise I'm afraid you'll lose interest in me and... and I'm afraid you'll want more, want someone else, that I won't be enough."

Her eyes are bright with unshed tears, her nose twitches, her lip trembles, she's on the verge of heartbreak. I should probably pull her tight against my chest so she can feel how strongly my heart beats and how my wolf purrs for her, but that's not my way.

Instead I sigh deeply saying: "Tő, Tő, Tő... you are my mate, my fated mate. I have married you, I have knotted you. I will never leave you and I won't let you leave me."

She half-laughs, half-sobs, calls me *Mr Romantic*, and ends up hiccuping. Blinking away her tears she smiles and stands up on her toes to kiss me. "*Szeretlek [I love you]*."

"*Ostoba lány, buta feleség [silly girl, foolish wife], én is szeretlek [I love you too]*."

"I had an interesting talk with Imre," Tó says, puzzling me even more since I thought the two of them hated each other.

"Remember the first time you contacted him and talked about getting his help to clear your name and all that? Well afterwards Imre called back and I answered your phone. You must have been in the shower.

Anyhow, he said he was calling because he'd had an idea. He knew we travel under false identities so he suggested why not keep them? He said *why not let the authorities think that you two are dead, casualties of the war with the Balázs pack, so they will drop the charges and you could go anywhere in the world under your new names?*

I didn't say anything at the time because I realized that would never work for you. You have to be free and clear of suspicion because you were driven away once before and couldn't - wouldn't - let that happen again. But now that you are cleared... we do have well-forged documents, we have money, and we really could go anywhere."

"So that's what you'd like to do? I know you've never had a chance to travel and there are places I'd like to show you, and places I'd like to see myself. We don't always have to go by plane since you hate flying. We could drive to Croatia and see Ilona and her new family!

We can do this Tó, if that's what you want?"

"Meeting your sister and traveling with you sounds wonderful, but Antal, what really matters is just the fact of being with you. It doesn't matter where we are so long as we're together. We can do anything and everything!"

"We can *die* and create scandalous headlines full of speculation while we're off having fun traveling incognito–"

"And sorry-not sorry if that makes trouble for the Royal Family!"

"Then, once the media has forgotten all about us we'll simply stroll back into our lives and be *utterly baffled* at all the confusion."

Tő's eyes light up with devilish excitement. "Can we really do this? Fuck, can we?"

Her enthusiasm makes me smile so I give the idea full consideration before answering: "Yes, we can. Of course my family and our friends will need to know the truth, they aren't going to be putting on a funeral, but maybe... hmm, maybe they can issue a statement saying they've been prohibited from discussing us? That will sound like the Royals are being heavy-handed and in full cover-up mode."

"I love-love-love it!" She shrieks excitedly. "We get to have fun doing exactly what *we* want while they suffer false accusations. Then we come home and create a whole new scandal!"

"Yes, *édesem [my darling]*, we'll come back in time for you to have a scandal for Christmas. Here we celebrate it for a couple of weeks and have a wonderful time. It's a great holiday to share with a pack. You'll love it."

Acknowledgement

Writing is a pleasurable challenge and I really appreciate that you've read my book. I hope you enjoyed it and will leave a review as this helps others decide if they'll like the book too.

I'd love to know your thoughts! please email me at: AuthorLoriLaidlaw@gmail.com

And read about upcoming releases on my website: https://lori-laidlaw-novelist-bvwonn.mailerpage.io/

Also by Lori Laidlaw

Lockdown + 3 Alphas = Heat: An Omega's Thrilling Dark Romantic Adventure

Girlie: Undeniable Attraction Enemies to Lovers Steamy Standalone

Cruel Obligation

Jane's Special Adventure

Captive's Deception

Finn and Marbeth

"Princess Weds Killer" = Fake News

Watch for more at https://lori-laidlaw-novelist-bvwonn.mailerpage.io/.

About the Author

Lori says:

I'm a bit shy... but I love reading and writing in the Adult Romance genre with all its sub-categories.

I fall in love with my characters whose moods range from playful to dangerous and everything in between!

My stories are multiple POV expressing mature themes and passionate encounters with enough steam to stimulate your imagination.

It's all about the love.

Email: AuthorLoriLaidlaw@gmail.com

Website: https://lori-laidlaw-novelist-bvwonn.mailerpage.io/

Facebook: https://www.facebook.com/people/ Author-Lori-Laidlaw/61555470454210/

Goodreads: https://www.goodreads.com/author/show/ 29566696.Lori_Laidlaw

Read more at https://lori-laidlaw-novelist-bvwonn.mailerpage.io/.

www.ingramcontent.com/pod-product-compliance
Lightning Source LLC
Chambersburg PA
CBHW020954180626
46814CB00003B/1081